Emily Lawless

Major Lawrence, F.L.S.

A Novel

Emily Lawless

Major Lawrence, F.L.S.
A Novel

ISBN/EAN: 9783337032623

Printed in Europe, USA, Canada, Australia, Japan

Cover: Foto ©Andreas Hilbeck / pixelio.de

More available books at **www.hansebooks.com**

BY THE

HON. EMILY LAWLESS,

AUTHOR OF "HURRISH: A STUDY," ETC.

IN THREE VOLUMES.

VOL. II.

LONDON:
JOHN MURRAY, ALBEMARLE STREET.

1887.

CONTENTS.

VOLUME II.

BOOK III.

BOOK IV.

BOOK III.

FIVE YEARS LATER.

MAJOR LAWRENCE, F.L.S.

CHAPTER I.

By the middle of November the flowers in
the Tuileries garden have naturally got into
their decadence. They are not, however,
even in that state plucked up by the roots
and hustled brutally away in wheel-barrows,
as are the summer plants of our own parks,
but are allowed to die naturally, harmlessly,
decently, each in its own appointed place.
One morning, a traveller, newly arrived in
Paris, lingered a few minutes to glance
over the still pretty but melancholy par-
terres of petunias and geraniums thus dying
leisurely upon their stalks, and over their
heads at the long line of acacias and plane-
trees, which also showed a somewhat

dejected mien; the former altogether de-
nuded, the latter festooned only with those
tenacious little button-like balls, which
long survive the leaves, and swing, no
matter how bad the weather, wild the wind,
hard the frost, until spring comes to loose
their thread-like strands, and set free their
imprisoned energies for the newly assigned
task of dissemination.

Our traveller—let us say at once Major
Lawrence—was not thinking of plane-trees
or their habits, though he might have done
so at another time. Having only just
arrived in Paris, there were naturally more
urgent matters than button-balls to lay
claims to his attention.

Oddly enough, he had never been there
before. Although in his time he had done
his fair share of travelling, it had always
been along one fixed route. He had always
sailed direct to India from Southampton,
without visiting other places than those
which lay unavoidably on his way. Now,
as upon former occasions, he was bound for

India, being due at the head-quarters of his
regiment at a certain date in early spring.
That date was still, however, remote, and
he proposed to fill up a part of the interval
by acquainting himself with those centres
of European civilization, which it is held
incumbent upon a man's self-respect to
have seen. He had only five minutes before come out of the Louvre, and was at
that moment asking himself with some
severity whether he had consciously or unconsciously carried away even one available
idea from that marvellous emporium of all
possible styles and schools, but was obliged,
after careful consideration, to own, with a
shake of the head, that he doubted it. And
so, with a half-smile over his own artistic
disabilities, and a glance at the charred
remains of what was once the palace of the
Tuileries, and which still then cumbered
the ground, he strolled away out of the
gardens, up the Rue de Rivoli, turning presently along the Rue Castiglione in the
direction of the Place Vendôme.

His history since the day we parted with
him will not take many words to relate.
He had gone to India, and had there devoted himself to such work as he found to
do, if not with any very gracious good-will,
at least with that dogged resolution which
stands our countrymen in place of more
attractive, but perhaps on the whole less
useful qualities. In the common course of
events he would have remained where he
was for several years longer. A call, however, had come which had decided him to
ask for leave sooner than he would otherwise have done.

Judge Lawrence had been stricken down
with a stroke of paralysis at the age of
seventy-six—in the flower, it seemed, of
his youth and vigour,—and, although the
first assault had not killed him, the doctors
could give little hope that his life would be
prolonged beyond a few months. The letter
which had brought this news brought also
an appeal from the stricken man that his
son John would, if by any possibility it

could be managed, come home. The said
son John had been a little surprised at the
urgency of this appeal, but had not seen fit
to disregard it. He had come home, and
was glad he had done so, as it seemed to
give his father a feeling of satisfaction to
see him sitting beside his bed, and to know
that, whatever happened, he was at hand.
The only other son available—William, the
Yorkshire parson—had always been regarded
in the family as a rather feckless and in-
vertebrate sort of being, not particularly
available, or to be relied upon in an emer-
gency.

It was a weary waiting through that
dreary month of September in the half-
empty town, where the roll of carriages
in the street below grew more and more
languid, until they seemed upon the point
of ceasing altogether. At last the end
came, the poor Judge slipping out of life
early one grey October morning, before
there was time for the nurse to summon
any one except John, who was dozing upon

a sofa in the next room. Then followed
the funeral, and all the other dreary
necessary arrangements, most of the ordering of which fell to our hero's share.
There had never been very much sympathy
between him and his stepmother, who had
early in their acquaintanceship pronounced
him, as we know, to be ponderous. Now,
however, in the shock of this sudden
bereavement, shaken out of her little social
phylacteries, astray amongst the grim
realities of life where good manners and
easy self-confidence were not of any immediate avail, the poor woman turned, not
without a sensation of relief, to this big
unexpansive step-son of hers, whose
shoulders were precisely of that build
ordained apparently by nature for bearing
any number of burdens that it might be
convenient to lay upon them. He made
all arrangements possible for her well-being,
and for that of the two small sisters, too
young, happily, to realize very clearly what
had happened. This done, he had gone

down to Colt's Head, proposing to spend a month or two upon his own little territory there, and perhaps to recreate himself a little over the old beloved pursuits.

As matters turned out he did not remain there as long as he had intended. The weather, for one thing, was atrocious, so that it had been impossible to think of dredging. Holes had come in the roof of the cottage, the woodwork of the doors and windows had grown warped by damp and neglect, the wind whistling through in icy splinters, chilling him to the bone as he sat at his study table. Perhaps he would have been able to hold out against these minor miseries had he found alleviation, as of yore, outside his own dominions, but this was not the case. Mordaunt was shut up, and its mistress abroad, and was at the present time settled temporarily in Paris.

He had received several letters from her since his return. In the last, a very kind one, which had reached him shortly after

his father's death, she had urged him to
leave England, and come and see her. It
would be very good for him, she felt sure,
after all he had gone through. There was
a piece of information towards the end of
this letter which had astonished Major
Lawrence very much, nay, had disturbed
him greatly—more so than he could have
believed any piece of news, not immediately
connected with his own family, could have
disturbed him at such a time. This
information was that his old playfellow
Elly Mordaunt, now nearly eighteen years
of age, was engaged to be married to *her*
old playfellow, young Mr. Algernon Cathers!

When for any reason we turn our backs
upon our native shore or native village, and
wander out into the great world, nothing
strikes us as so preposterous upon our
return as the conduct of the children. The
babies whom we left in arms, and who now
look up in our faces responsible beings who
know their Catechisms; the boys who were
playing pegtop, and who now know so much

more than we do ourselves, who have
grown so wise, so far-sighted, who are
capable of giving us such excellent advice!
The Major, albeit a reasonable man, was
not more exempt from this form of folly
than another. To his perceptions Elly
Mordaunt was still precisely twelve years
old; an agile, colt-like creature, with long
active limbs, not too much embarrassed
with drapery; with grey, keenly inquisitive
eyes, always widely opened; with a mutinous little mouth, prompt to utter audacious
sayings; with a dense crest of brown hair
rising up from her forehead, and hanging in
a tangled mane over her shoulders. Do
what he would, it was impossible for him to
conceive her under any other guise. That
she should be a young lady—grown up,
decorous, prettily behaved—seemed impossible; that any one should talk of her
getting married, preposterous and unnatural; but that she should be actually
engaged, and engaged to Algernon Cathers
of all people upon earth, struck him with a

cold chill, a dull sense of the anomalous and the incongruous, which he could hardly himself account for.

Apparently Lady Mordaunt—whose first mention of the subject, necessarily short, had been speedily followed by a letter in which it had been dwelt upon at greater length—did not regard it herself with any particular complacency. *She* had had no hand in it, she assured him, in fact, until the news reached her a week before, no glimmering of such a notion had even distantly visited her imagination. It was a confession of stupidity, she admitted, but so it was. No doubt the young people had seen a good deal of one another. She had had Elly with her last winter at Mentone, where the Cathers' villa was one of the show things of the place. Young Cathers had been there, as he always was at that time of year, and had been attentive—very attentive—but as to the smallest symptom of any return upon her grand-daughter's side, she had not seen the ghost of a

fraction. Flirtation was an accomplish-
ment which Elly showed no disposition to
acquire, and as for anything more serious,
she would as soon have expected her to
fall in love with the knob of the nearest
weather-cock. However, that the thing
was an accomplished fact there was, unfortunately, no doubt. In the end it must
have been settled very suddenly. The
young people had met again in the spring
at Florence, where Elly had gone with her
mother, and afterwards at Homburg, where
the final understanding had come about.
How it had been achieved, whether pressure
had been brought to bear upon the girl by
her mother, or whether the young man had
gone down upon his knees and threatened
there and then to break a blood-vessel—he
was supposed to be consumptive—unless
she took pity on him, was more than she
could say. It was not, he could imagine,
a question that could be put in a letter.
She expected to see Elly and her mother
shortly, as they were to pass through Paris

on their way to Mentone, and she would then be in a better position to judge how far it was the girl's own doing, and how far she had been egged into it by others.

Plenty of people, Lady Mordaunt went on to observe, would tell you that it was an excellent marriage. The Cathers were nobodies, rather less than nobodies, this young man's grandfather having, she believed, arrived in London with the traditional half-crown in his pocket. Only retrograde old fogies, however, like herself, troubled their heads about such things now-a-days. If a man had money enough, who cared where, how, or in what fashion it had been picked up? This young man, it was supposed, would have between forty and fifty thousand a year when he came of age, which would be in a little more than a twelvemonth's time. He was quite presentable too, no doubt, and had the manners of a gentleman—so at least everybody seemed to consider. He was even supposed to be clever, though she was

bound to say that she had never perceived
any particular symptoms of it herself. He
collected orchids, she knew, and she
believed teapots, and sang a little, and
painted a little, and discoursed about Art
more than a little, and was undoubtedly
a very striking young man to look at in
the Romanesque and melodramatic style.
Which of these various attractions and
accomplishments, or whether all of them
combined, had attracted her grand-
daughter's affections, was more than she
could say. To so old a friend as himself—
one whose discretion she could depend
upon—she would not hesitate to say that
she was disappointed, even bitterly disappointed. She had always believed that
Elly had a soul above teapots, and that
the meretricious attractions of a little self-
satisfied *petit-maitre* were the last that
would have won her heart. One lived and
learned, however! There was nothing in
which old people showed their folly more
conspicuously than in thinking that they

knew anything about the young people
with whom they lived. You saw them go
in and out; you heard every word they
uttered; you fancied you could peep into
their very souls. And one fine day—piff
paff!—you find that you know no more
about them than if they were a set of young
paroquets, and you an old blind buzzard!
Meanwhile garrulity was evidently gaining
upon her, which was another proof of
dotage, and she would therefore only add
that she hoped sincerely he would take her
advice and come to Paris, where, if she
could promise him nothing else, she could
at least assure him of a very hearty greeting
from his affectionate old friend, Georgina
F. Mordaunt.

The Major was thinking about this letter
as he walked along the street, throwing a
glance from time to time at the marvels
of the goldsmith's art which gleamed and
glittered at him from the shop windows.
He did not like the idea of this marriage
one whit better than Lady Mordaunt,

indeed, it seemed to him that the tone she took about it was altogether too light for the occasion, that some much more serious and strenuous effort ought to be made to hinder such a consummation from taking place.

His life upon the other side of the globe had been so absolutely apart from his life in England that everything that had taken place before his last departure stood out with a vividness and sharpness which it certainly would not have possessed had the continuity of his days never been broken. There was hardly an incident of which he did not remember everything, down to the minutest particular. As regards Mordaunt, and all that had taken place in or near it, this retrospective vision was particularly clear. His recollection of Elly Mordaunt herself was, as has been said, even inconveniently so, seeing that it must soon give place to what in all probability would be an utterly different one. He had only to shut his eyes and there she was—grey eyes,

tossed hair, mutinous mouth, short skirts—
all complete as in a picture !

His recollection of her occasional play-
mate, Algernon Cathers, was hardly less
vivid. Without even troubling himself to
shut his eyes, he could see him ; the
narrow handsome face ; the clear-cut regular
features—too regular and clear-cut by far
for his age—the great sombre eyes ; the
unboylike look of superciliousness and suspicion. He had been a nasty upsetting
little imp, in his elder acquaintance's candid
opinion, puffed up with his prospective possessions, and the idolatry of an idiotic
mother. A purse-proud man is bad enough,
but a purse-proud boy is revolting ! He
had not even, in his critic's eyes, those
compensating qualities which are supposed
to belong to the type. He had been a little
coward, and a little liar, and it was that
prejudiced person's opinion that he would
in all probability prove to be a larger
coward, and a larger liar now. He was
not so lost to self-knowledge as to be un-

unaware that, like many other excellent people, he was given to taking prejudices, and that for one reason or another he had taken an unusually vehement one against young Master Cathers. From Lady Mordaunt's description—a portrait drawn avowedly by no partial hand—it was evident that he must have altered considerably, and altered, no doubt, for the better. Let him have altered as much as he would he had no business, in our hero's opinion, to have been allowed so much as to dream of marrying Elly Mordaunt. There are moral and mental traits as unalterable as the shape of the eyes or the colour of the skin, traits which no amount of scouring could remove. Though no stickler either for rank and position—rather inclining to democratic views than otherwise—his feeling was that there was something about the case which savoured not remotely of presumption—the sort of presumption which called for summary chastisement.

The bare thought of those two together

filled his mind with angry astonishment.
She *must* have been egged into it, he
thought, she would never surely have made
such a choice of her own free will? And
yet again his recollections of Elly Mordaunt
did not present her as a favourable subject
for compulsion, especially at the hands of
the Countess her mother; added to which
he had an uncomfortable recollection that
she had by no means shared his view of
Algernon Cathers, even in those bygone
days. Women, he reflected — and little
Elly Mordaunt, odd as the words sounded,
was a woman now—were proverbially unaccountable, and in no respect more start-
lingly, disagreeably unaccountable than in
the beings whom they select to expend
their affections upon.

Meanwhile he was getting rather tired
of the subject, which had occupied his mind
with tiresome persistency ever since he first
heard of it. He was tired too, as new
arrivals in Paris are apt to be, of the endless babble and clatter, the eye-wearying

brilliancy and glitter of its streets. Seeing
therefore a flight of steps in the distance,
he made for them. They led, he found,
to the doorway of a church. He did not
trouble himself to look for its name, nor
yet to push aside the rather uninviting-
looking brown curtain which hung before
the doorway, but seated himself outside
in an angle where a low wall afforded a
seat, and where a projecting buttress of
masonry made a convenient shelter against
the wind.

His India-nurtured blood felt comforted
by the warmth of the sunshine, now he
could get it without the cutting blast which
had met him at every corner of the street
below, and he stayed there for some time,
sunning himself on the steps, smoking his
cigar, and watching the kaleidoscope varieties of Parisian life which presented themselves upon the asphalte below. A funeral
cortège happened to be passing, and attracted his attention. He was not aware
that funerals constitute one of the per-

quisites of Government, but the fashion in
which it was conducted commended itself
to his approbation. The black car, despite
some unnecessary bedizenment, was certainly an improvement upon that mon-
strosity of wooden pegs and grimy feathers,
within which the subject of the British
Crown is conveyed to his last home. The
official, too, with the cocked hat, black
stockings and a sword, who walked before
the chief mourners, might be a trifle ridiculous, but he also was surely an improvement
upon the preposterous being in cotton gloves
and crape weepers who serves our countrymen as the emblem of official woe.

Though cold, the day was brilliant, and
Paris that morning was at her freshest,
with a certain air of youthfulness and guile-
lessness about her splashing fountains and
evergreen-decked squares, which those inti-
mately acquainted with that mature en-
chantress 'find not a little diverting. The
Major was not at all acquainted with her,
but he, too, was considerably diverted. He

had a commendable desire, moreover, to improve his knowledge—to steep himself, as it were, in the Parisian elixir—and in pursuance of this desire presently plunged down sundry dark-looking alleys, and up and down numerous steep flights of stairs, with the result of after a while losing his way, and having to appeal to the charity of passers-by, generally stout dames with baskets on their arms, who, mollified by his politeness, took pity upon him, and conducted him back to the regions of the recognizable.

In pursuance of the same idea he also travelled half over Paris upon a succession of omnibuses, taking tickets at a multiplicity of offices for places whose very names were utterly unknown to him. Lady Mordaunt had named five o'clock as the hour at which he was to call at her hotel, and he had therefore abundance of time in which to pursue these interesting and original investigations. That tinge of democratic sentiment which had survived his Indian experiences, was

not a little edified by that fine republican
admixture of which these vehicles constitute
the visible and recognized embodiment.
The ladies in velvets and sables, and the
ladies in cotton skirts and pleated caps;
the gentlemen in superfine broadcloth, and
the gentlemen in patched boots and blue
blouses, the gentlemen of the latter denomi-
nation sitting luxuriously too, in all the
dignity of possession, and the gentlemen of
the former standing upon the step of the
vehicle, or clutching frantically at the woodwork to hinder themselves from being pre-
cipitated into the street. Chivalry he
observed to be somewhat at a discount, more
so even than in a London omnibus, and
when upon one occasion he ceded his place
to a stout lady, who, unable to find one, had
stood helplessly in front of him, swaying like
a captive balloon with every movement of
the vehicle, he observed a gleam of sudden
astonishment steal irresistibly over the faces
of his fellow-travellers.

In due time he reached Lady Mordaunt's

hotel, and was shown by a waiter to her
apartment, which was upon the second floor.
It was a pretty little suite of rooms, with a
great deal of gilding, and no less than six
curtains, four thick and two thin to every
window. In spite of these defences, and of
the sunlight which was streaming in a thin
but vivid streak along one of the walls, he
found his old friend upon her knees before a
small stove, trying with a pair of bellows to
induce some logs of wood to emit a blaze,
and the first words she addressed to him
were a complaint of the cold.

"I am reduced to the position of a
stoker!" she exclaimed tragically, seating
herself with an air of exhaustion in an armchair and allowing him to take the bellows
out of her hand and apply himself to the
task. "If I allow my attention to be
diverted ten minutes from those ridiculous
morsels of wood the room becomes an
ice-house. Thank Heaven, I shall not have
much more of it! Next Tuesday I start for
Mentone. And you? How are you? Put

that implement down and let me look at you. You are not looking at all well, do you know; not at all. You are very thin, you look a great deal older than you have any right to do. Well, well, I forgot, perhaps it is not to be wondered at. You will get better after a while, no doubt. And your plans—what are they? Sit down there and tell me everything—everything."

The Major, who had by this time succeeded in inducing the semblance of an illumination to break out over the surface of the logs, laid down his bellows and turned to face his friend. Five years had made less difference in her than it had in him. Her eyes were not less blue, or less bright than formerly, and though the lines around them might have deepened a little here and there, her face upon the whole had gained in placidity during the interval. That nobility of ex-pression, which was always its reigning characteristic, was deepened, too, rather than impaired by the lapse of years. She might amuse herself with grumbling, but

one had a feeling that it was mainly superficial. The deepest deeps were rarely
disturbed.

"My plans?" he said, replying to the
question easiest answered. "As usual they
are of the most eminently prosaic description. I am simply going back to India.
Only upon this occasion I am not going
there quite direct. I have two months
before I need sail, and after paying my
respects to you, I was thinking of trying to
improve my mind a little. You have always
told me that I was an utter barbarian in
matters of Art, so I am going now to try and
let in a little light in that direction. I was
thinking of going to Florence and Rome,
then, if I have any time left, to Naples,
where I propose relaxing my mind exhausted
by so much art, over the zoologic station
there. After which I am afraid it will be
time to take the steamer for Alexandria."

"So! You have laid out quite a neat
little programme for yourself, have you not?
Only, my dear friend, my very, *very* dear

friend, let me modify it a little. Come first
to Mentone! Remember how long it is
since I have seen you. Surely you owe
me a little of your time? Will you escort
me there on Tuesday next? Say yes!
You would, if you only knew what a true
kindness to me your doing so would be."

He hesitated a little. "There is nothing
in the world I should like better, of course,"
he said slowly. "Only—— "

"Only what?"

"Well, I had not thought of staying in
Paris so long, for one thing."

"Long! To-day is Wednesday; there
are only six days, therefore, till next Tuesday. You don't mean to tell me that
any young man in the world would be
at a loss to occupy himself for six days in
Paris?"

"I suppose not."

"Of course not. And you talk of Art!
Come to-morrow and I will introduce you
to a delightful young man, a particular
favourite of mine, who will put you com-

pletely *au courant*. He has the whole
world of modern French art at his finger's
end ; literally at his finger's end."

" I have been to the Louvre ! " the Major
replied in a tone of self-justification.

" The Louvre ! What is the Louvre ?
Tourists go there ! M. Alaric Brown will
take you to any studio you wish. He
knows all the artists, from Jérôme himself
downwards."

" I don't think, if I remained, it would be
on that account."

" Well, remain upon my account; that
will be infinitely better. You have no idea
what it is to me to see you, or what a
disappointment it would be to lose sight of
you again so soon. Promise, too, that you
will come to Mentone. I only wish I could
ask you to come to my own little abode
there, but it is a scrap, hardly fit for even
one reasonably sized human being to in-
habit. My daughter-in-law and grand-
daughter, too, are already there. They
went on before me last week. There is an

hotel, however, close by, where—knowing
your unsociable ways—I have no doubt you
will be much happier, and whence you will
condescend to come and see me from time
to time. Don't refuse. Believe me, I need
a little consolation. You will find Elly,
too. You have not forgotten little Elly,
have you? Big Elly—she has grown a
giantess." There were no more direct
allusions to recent events."

The Major replied gravely that he had
not at all forgotten Elly. Nevertheless he
hesitated. There were many things which
induced him to fall in with this programme,
but there were others which made it singularly distasteful, the very charm of those
earlier associations making him shrink fan-
tastically from imperilling them. In the
end, however, he gratified Lady Mordaunt
by agreeing to do what she wished; pro-
mising to remain in Paris until the following
Tuesday, and to escort her then to Mentone, leaving the duration of his stay to be
determined by future considerations. After

all, it was always upon the road to Italy, he
reflected, and he need not remain an hour
longer than he liked.

Next day he called again, according to
her orders, and was introduced to M. Alaric
Brown, who amiably offered to call for him
upon the following afternoon at any hour
he liked after three o'clock, and inoculate
him, as far as so crude a disciple could
be inoculated in so short a time, into the
mysteries of Parisian Art.

M. Alaric Brown was a short, rather
stout, but particularly alert young gentleman, who condescended to occupy a stool
in a Government office, but whose real
predilections were for the Fine Arts, which
he cultivated in his leisure hours, and
which his friends assured him only required
further assiduity upon his part in order to
place him quite in the first rank of con-
temporary talent. Over and above this
proof of genius, his two chief sources of
self-congratulation were his English birth
and his profound acquaintanceship with the

world of Paris. Brown undoubtedly is an English name, and M. Alaric Brown's grandfather had been an Englishman who had married and settled in France. His son, however, had forsworn that side of his nationality, which had lapsed into oblivion until revived by the grandson, who found it in some respects advantageous to his status as a man of fashion. He dressed in the height of English tailoring—as English tailoring is understood in Paris—was authoritative upon sport, as an Englishman was bound to be ; kept a large collection of whips and walking-sticks in his apartments ; likewise a bull-dog which he called "Billee," and of which he was evidently afraid.

Under the guidance of this accomplished young gentleman, the Major was taken to several exhibitions which had recently opened their doors to a discriminating public. The first of these was a very sumptuous affair, approached through ante- chambers abounding in plush-covered sofas,

and watched over by attendants in satin
knee-breeches with gold lace upon the
sleeves of their coats. The other was in
a narrower street, and was, his guide in-
formed him, more "modest" altogether.
Judging by the first delineation of the
human form which met his eye the Major
felt a little inclined to cavil at the correct-
ness of the epithet, but in the end let it
pass unchallenged. His new acquaintance
also took him to the studios of various
artists, with whom he appeared to be upon
terms of considerable intimacy, and who all
joked him about his artistic achievements,
which seemed to be a recognized subject of
studio banter. From the conversation of
these gentlemen, and M. Brown's comments
thereon, our hero was enlightened upon a
good many details with regard to what may
be called the backstairs regions of con-
temporary art, some of which astonished
him not a little. Indeed, on not a few
points, social as well as artistic, M. Brown's
remarks were a revelation to him, a fact

which evidently gave no slight satisfaction
to that well-informed young gentleman, who
was not insensible to the glory of acting as
pioneer and exponent of the Parisian mysteries to a personage who, however distinguished in his own line, was confessedly
in such matters a mere infant in arms as
compared with himself.

If his first impression was one of abounding variety, our Major's last impression of
Paris was one of decided and, as it appeared
to him, oppressive monotony. Before the
five days which he had promised to wait for
Lady Mordaunt were over, he felt that he
had seen enough of it. It seemed to him—
very absurdly of course—as if of late he had
seen nothing but endless repetitions of the
same things; the same eternal many-storied
white houses; the same entrances, with the
same dingy curtains, and the same cross-
faced woman in the same smart cap; the
same *cafés* with the same *garçons;* the same
gentlemen drinking coffee or absinthe, and
glancing with the same air of leisurely

impertinence at the passers-by; the same caricatures in half a hundred print shops; the same superficial intelligence in half a thousand faces. In every theatre—and he made a point of going to a different one each evening—the same plots, the same jests, the same perpetual and, as it seemed to him, wearisome iterations, upon the same well-worn themes. What did astonish him was the ever fresh interest shown by those about him in what to him in so brief a period had already become threadbare. Knowing no better explanation, he set it down provisionally to the score of Gallic frivolity. They had probably nothing better to do! he reflected.

According to previous agreement he met Lady Mordaunt upon the Tuesday morning at the Gare de Lyon, and they travelled south together.

It had turned grey as well as cold in Paris the last few days, which added to the unfavourable impression with which that capital of all conceivable delights had inspired him. This coldness and greyness pursued them during the earlier part of their journey, and seemed to gather intensity at Lyons, which was viewed through the unbecoming medium of a violent snowstorm. The sun, however, which to their perceptions had never risen at all, went down with dazzling splendour behind the blistered hills of Provence, and when next morning they awoke in Marseilles, where upon Lady Mordaunt's account they had decided upon sleeping, it was upon a Mediterranean blue as tradition herself could inspire, upon a horizon which glowed and quivered with superfluous sunshine, upon all that matchless combination of light, life, colour, vegetation, which in winter makes that thirteen hours' journey the most effective bit of travelling to be found, probably, upon the face of the earth.

It was dark by the time they reached Mentone, and having seen Lady Mordaunt started to her villa, which was at some distance from the railway, the Major had

barely time to reach his hotel in order to
make one of a meagre and rather discon-
solate-looking company, chiefly of elderly
ladies, gathered round one end of an enormously long table, which stretched itself in
gloomy but prophetic fashion the entire
length of the apartment. Late as the hour
was, one of the windows was open, and in
the intervals of his neighbours' chirping, he
could hear the grinding roll of the surf, as
it picked up all the loose stones and pebbles
within reach, carried them in for some
distance upon its shoulders, and then, with
a sudden impulse of petulance, flung them
down noisily upon the shore again. He
walked a little while along the edge of this
same querulous sea afterwards, and smelt
its fragrance, which did not strike him as
ambrosial, and looked at the twinkling
galaxies of light, set, like so many stunted
candelabra, at intervals along the nearly
invisible line of coast. Then it grew chilly,
and he went indoors, and shortly afterwards
to bed, where he dreamed that he was walk-

ing by himself along the shore near Colt's
Head, and that a large fish lay stranded
there, of a species unknown, it seemed
to him, to science. And that he hurried to
the spot to secure it, but when he came
near, he saw to his astonishment and dis-
comfiture that it was no other than that
anatomically impossible creature a mermaid,
for in its hand it held a comb, and from its
head fell a quantity of light brown hair.
And he tried to catch it, wondering, as he
did so, what in the world Professor Jenkyll
would say when he saw it; but it foiled
him and darted away like a thing of quick-
silver into the water. And just as it was
disappearing under the surface it turned
suddenly round with a laugh upon its face,
and then he saw that it was no other than
little Elly Mordaunt!

CHAPTER II.

HE thought of his dream when he awoke
next morning, and laughed a little over it.
It certainly stimulated his curiosity to see
her again, which was already sufficiently
lively. He could not well intrude upon
Lady Mordaunt before four o'clock in the
afternoon he thought, not knowing that
upon the Riviera all social institutions are
ante-dated at least an hour. He spent the
interval in wandering about and getting
acquainted with this gay little sanatorium
into which he had dropped. As far as he
could see, there were not many signs of
mortality about. Here and there some pale
or flushed face looked up at him out of
bath-chairs, and from sheltered nooks in

the corners of the cliff, but the general
effect was cheerful enough. The masses of
flowers were really surprising. The autumn
rains, as it happened, had that season been
a little late, and everything which had been
waiting impatiently for their coming had
burst into sudden blossom. It seemed as
if the 20th of November was quite the recognized moment for the opening of the
floral season.

Towards four o'clock he directed his
steps to Lady Mordaunt's villa, the position
of which he had ascertained the previous
evening. As its mistress had declared, it
was certainly a diminutive abode. It stood
by itself in the midst of a small and excessively steep strip of garden, which was
approached from the road through a white
gate, upon the posts of which the name—
" Les Avants "—appeared in black paint.
A very bright little garden it was, that
wealth of vegetation which had already
taken him by surprise, and which seemed
to fling defiance at the almanac, being well

represented here. There were roses, red,
yellow, and white ; creepers of varieties
unknown to him dangled about from wall
and branch, and as he was passing upwards
a great fragrant mass of yellow mimosa
swung itself with a sort of bluff hospitality
right across his face.

The house, or cottage, stood upon an
artificially levelled piece of ground cut out
of the rock, which rose behind it like a wall,
encircled and apparently supported at the
base by a green-latticed enclosure, also
over-climbed by creepers. All the doors
and windows opening upon the gravel, the
Major felt some little doubt as to which of
these apertures was intended to be approached by visitors, but at last decided in
favour of one which was already partially
open, and to the side of which hung a bell-
handle attached to the inside wall by a
twisted chain.

This handle he pulled, without, however,
producing any sound; pulled it again, and
again waited, but still no one came, nothing

happened.   He was about to essay it a
third time, when his attention was arrested
by a sound of singing from the rock immediately above his head, followed by a
light noise of falling sand and pebbles, and
the footsteps of some one approaching.

He looked up, and—exactly as in the
opening scene of an opera—saw a young
man about to descend a nearly perpen-
dicular flight of steps hewn out of the rock,
singing to himself as he did so.   If anything the appearance of this young man
was rather more suggestive of the stage
than was the mode of his approach.   He
was not, it is true, arrayed like a trouba-
dour or a Greek god, his legs were not
bare, and he neither carried a crook nor
balanced a thyrsus, but had he done either
of these things, he could hardly, in the ultra-
Britannic eyes of our Major, have looked less
like an ordinary visitor, and more like a
vision from the operatic boards.   His head,
defined against the deep blue of the sky
behind, was covered with a flat cap of dull

orange hue, his clothes were light coloured, his collar, which was loose, was tied with a necktie of the same colour as his cap, and in his hand he carried a mass of some brilliantly scarlet, tropical-looking flower, which flung back over his shoulder, stood out in audacious splendour full against the sky.

The young man's face, moreover, was even more striking than his clothes, his burden, or his background. It seemed difficult to conceive that anything so realistic of the dreams of love-lorn maidens was to be found in solid every-day flesh and blood. Had the Appollino, or Paris as first beheld by Helen, taken it into their [heads to appear in modern guise in a Mentonese garden, they would doubtless have presented some such appearance as that presented by the young man who was at that moment descending Lady Mordaunt's steps.

The Major—who being no better-looking than his neighbours, had a natural disdain for exceptional masculine beauty—settled

it in his own mind that the new-comer must
be an Italian, probably a singer, dancer,
painter, or something of that sort, wondering as he did so what the deuce the impudent
jackanapes meant by coming to call upon
ladies in that free-and-easy fashion ?

He had plenty of time to observe the
phenomenon, as, in spite of another indig-
nant pull at the bell, no one came near the
door.   Upon his side the young man overhead seemed in no particular hurry to
descend, but came leisurely down step by
step, humming, and looking about him with
a smile as he did so.   Upon the last flight,
however, he made a halt, and his eyes, which
had hitherto been roving over the garden,
suddenly concentrated themselves upon the
figure at the door.   Hardly had he done so,
before, interrupting himself in the middle of
a bar, he ran down the remaining steps, and
up to the surprised John Lawrence, his hand
outstretched in friendly greeting.

"My *dear* Major !   Why, of course, it must
be you !   How stupid of me not to think of

it immediately! How are you? Don't
stay pulling at that ridiculous chain. The
bell, if there ever was a bell, has been taken
down long ago. There is an electric one
somewhere or other, but the creepers have
got hold of it and smothered it. We won't
stop to look for it, however, but come round
to the drawing-room window. Excuse my
arms being so full. This is a new Nicar-
aguan creeper which has come out for the
first time, that I am bringing in triumph to
show Lady Elly. Isn't it sumptuous?"

While this explanation was going on, the
Major had time to collect his wits and to
realize who was speaking to him. He had
done so, in fact, almost at the first word.
The handsome man was not so utterly
unlike the handsome boy that, upon a nearer
view, he had any difficulty in recognizing
Algernon Cathers. The greatest change—
a change amounting to a transformation—
was the difference of expression. In place
of that supercilious distrust which had
made the boy's face, with all its beauty,

almost repulsive, the man's face seemed to
exhale good-humour and geniality at every
pore. There was an air of fragility about
him which argued, perhaps, no great vital
force. Even with this qualification, however, the first impulse of any unprejudiced
spectator would have been sheer admiration, if not something like involuntary
envy, at so brilliant an embodiment of
youth, prosperity, and masculine good looks
at the very highest point of their respective
attainment.

Major Lawrence, as we know, could hardly
be called an unprejudiced spectator, yet even
he was taken by surprise, not so much by
the young man's good looks, as by the quite
unlooked-for exhibition of cordiality towards
himself. Feeling, as he did, no great kindness towards young Mr. Cathers, feeling that
had he had the power of doing so, that
brilliant young gentleman would have been
sent to the right-about with the shortest
possible delay, it was perhaps natural that
he should have made up his mind that this

unamiable sentiment would be returned by its recipient, as it certainly had been in more youthful days. Apparently it was not so. Whatever animosity the boy Cathers might have cherished, the man Cathers had evidently forgotten all about it, and was prepared to be as friendly as an adopted son of the house was bound to be to one of its oldest friends.

No one was in the sitting-room when they entered, so the bell was rung, and in answer to young Mr. Cathers' inquiry, a maid who appeared said that Lady Mordaunt would be down in a few minutes, and that Lady Eleanor, she believed, was in the garden.

" In the garden? Then I think, if you'll excuse me, Major, I'll go out and look for her. To tell you the honest truth," he added, with a laugh, as the maid left the room, " I shake in my shoes whenever I am left alone with Lady Mordaunt, without Elly or her mother to protect me. I know the dear old lady privately wishes me at Jericho ! Addio, for the moment," and before the

Major had time to answer had he intended to do so, the young man had vanished through the window.

He had hardly disappeared before the door opened and Lady Mordaunt came in. She glanced round the room with an air of surprise as she shook hands with her guest. "Alone?" she said. "I thought I heard voices as I came down the stairs?"

"You did. Your—— Young Cathers was here. He has just gone through that window into the garden."

"You may finish your sentence—my grandson-elect, I suppose that was what you were going to say? There is no use blinking the matter, seeing that he is accepted, and it is therefore out of our hands, and no wishing or not wishing will avail to undo it. Well, what do you think of him now that you have seen him?" she went on, settling herself as she spoke in a corner of the sofa, and administering a corrective thump to one of the cushions before placing it behind her back.

" He appears a good deal improved—in— well, in appearance," the Major said with a gulp.

"Improved in appearance! Merciful powers! Is *that* all you can find to say? Improved in appearance! Why, he was always about a hundred times too good-looking!"

" He used to look so sullen, I mean. Now he looks beaming, satisfied, a perfect picture of amiability."

" Hump! Odd that he should be satisfied, isn't it?" Lady Mordaunt gave another corrective thump to her sofa-cushion. "What do most people require, I should like to know, to satisfy them? If to be rich enough to gratify every idiotic fancy you take into your head; if to be twenty years of age, and as vain and handsome as a peacock; if to be going to be married to a girl who is about a hundred thousand times too good for you; if all that doesn't make a man satisfied, all I can say is—— Why, Elly! I didn't know you were in the house. Zelie said you had gone into the garden."

John Lawrence sprang from his chair with a feeling of keen excitement as the young girl entered. She was very tall, taller even than she had promised to be, but his first impression was that she had not quite kept to her youthful promise of beauty. He was not disappointed exactly, still he made a mental note of the fact. Her face, it is true, had wonderfully little changed, so little that there would have been no question about recognizing her wherever and whenever they might have met. Her grey eyes had their old widely-opened look of enquiry, their old straightforward cordial expression, and her hair, in defiance of fashion, was brushed up as of yore from her forehead, and gathered into a loose knot at the back. In other respects she was certainly changed. Her expression was less confident, more reserved, and her mouth had quite lost those little mutinous, mirth-provoking curves, which

had been so characteristic of the child Elly.
So completely had this formed part of his
mental vision of her, that the absence of
it seemed to her old friend to leave a vague
sense of want and incompleteness. Her
figure was still rather angular, and, tall as
she was, she looked as if she might yet be
growing. She would not probably have
been pronounced at first sight, or by a
casual observer, a particularly pretty girl,
yet there was a certain maidenly stateliness
about her, which, combined with an air of
alertness, gave character and individuality
to her looks and even a certain dignity to
her shyness. Elly the child had been
totally free from shyness, but Elly the
maiden, as the Major at once perceived with
surprise, was certainly shy, and this shyness lent a restraint, and, as he afterwards
found, an occasional touch of awkwardness
to her manner. It did not, however, prevent her from coming forward now with all
her old cordiality to greet him.

"I am so glad you have come, so very

very glad," she said, and her truth-telling eyes echoed the sentiment to the uttermost.

"And I am very glad to find myself here, and to see you again," he replied; and then there was a pause as they mutually looked at each other.

"You have not altered, Lady Elly!" he said consideringly.

"Not altered?" she echoed with a sort of dismay. "Not altered?"

"Not much. You have grown a woman, of course; but your face is just the same."

"So I tell her," her grandmother joined in from the sofa. "Why she should object so particularly to the information I cannot imagine!"

"Because—only because—I thought I *had* altered," the girl said, turning away a little, as if embarrassed. There was another momentary pause, which was broken by Lady Mordaunt.

"That young man of yours is out there looking for you," she said drily. "It seems Zelie had told him you were in the garden."

" Did she ? Then if she said so perhaps
I had better go," her grand-daughter answered, without, however, immediately proceeding to do so.

" I can't, of course, engage that he is
there still. The garden is not of colossal
dimensions, and he can hardly have been all
this time discovering that you were not
in it. Possibly he may have gone again,
finding that—— "

" No he has not; he is here," said a
voice at the window, and young Mr. Cathers
entered, taking off his orange cap with a
graceful sweep as he did so. " Good-morn-
ing, Lady Mordaunt; I hope you are rested
after your journey ? I found Major Lawrence pulling at that brazen impostor outside the door, so took the liberty of bringing
him in through the window. Then led by a
false report of Zelie's, I went out, and was
wandering disconsolately along the edge of
your territory, when I was pounced upon
by that portentous old bore, Marjoribanks,
who discoursed to me for a quarter of an

hour about some universal Rivieran petition
he insists upon presenting to the French
Government, placing before them the hein-
ousness of their conduct in not forthwith
abolishing Monte Carlo, etcetera! He
wants, it seems, everybody's signature, and
especially yours, and called upon me to get
it for him. I modestly suggested that he
would do better to appeal to you himself,
but he seemed to think he could accomplish
some end by continuing to maunder on
upon the subject to me. I was despairing
of escaping, when by good luck some one
else came along the road, and my old man
of the sea rushed madly away in pursuit,
and I escaped. Come and see something I
have left outside in the verandah for you,"
he added, in a quick aside to Elly, who was
near him. " Don't you want to see what it
is ? " he added beseechingly. " Please *say*
you do ! "

She coloured a little, but moved without
hesitation towards the window, and they
went out together.

"I've made up my mind about one thing," Lady Mordaunt said in a tone of intense irritation as the two figures disappeared round the corner. " So I may as well tell it you at once.'

"And that is?" the Major said inquiringly.

" Simply that she is in love with him ; but *excessively* in love with him! There can be no question about it. None! "

" What makes you think that? You didn't seem to think so in Paris? " he asked quickly.

" Everything! nothing! The things she says, the things she doesn't say; the way she looks, the way she doesn't look; I hadn't seen them together, remember, for nearly a year. No, there's no use in our disguising the truth from ourselves, it will not only be an eminently successful marriage from a worldly point of view, but it will be a—*love-match!* " and Lady Mordaunt dropped her two hands and opened their palms widely, with the air of one who announces some utterly crushing disaster.

John Lawrence made no answer, but the gloom of his face more than reflected hers. "If it is to be, I suppose one ought to rejoice that it is so?" he said at last, gloomily.

"*You* may rejoice as much as you choose! I entirely decline to do anything of the sort. If it were not her own doing I could face it better. Something might happen. There would always be a hope that it might be broken off. As it is, nothing short of an earthquake or a providential pestilence, that I can see, will avail to rid us of him!"

"He seems to be—well—very amiably intentioned," the Major said, heroically.

"Amiably intentioned! He is abominably amiably intentioned! He is amiability itself in a coat and a pair of trousers! He was here for an hour last night, and made himself quite detestably agreeable. He possesses all the social attributes; he is an Antinous, and an Admirable Crichton rolled in one! I assure you his conversation was perfectly dazzling; it had all the sparkle and brilliancy of a Palais Royal ornament. Oh, he is a delightful young man!" and Lady Mordaunt took up her sofa-cushion again by the two corners, and shook it vindictively.

Half an hour later the Major was returning through the garden on his way to the hotel. He looked for the two young people, but failed to see anything of them. A little further on, however, he was passing under a wall, beyond which extended a piece of waste ground, as yet unbuilt over, and studded at close intervals with large olive-trees. Under the vapourous shadow of one of these he caught sight of the two he was in search of, she seated upon a low wall, he upon a large loose rock at her feet. The young man's face was upturned and laughing, his white teeth gleamed brilliantly as he talked; evidently some excellent jest was the subject of his discourse. The other face did not appear to be entirely responsive

to this humorous appeal. It was sober to
seriousness, the grey eyes looking downwards
with an expression almost of disapproval.
Suddenly, however, the disapproval, if disapproval it were, seemed to lift, melt, and
vanish away.   More and more the face
softened; an expression half-reluctant, half-
admiring, wholly tender and loving, irradiat-
ing it like a ray of sunlight.   The Major
turned away with a sense of unendurable
disgust and kicked a large pebble which
happened to be lying near his foot into the
sea.   There was no question about it, he
said to himself savagely.   Lady Mordaunt
was perfectly right.   It would be a love-
match!

CHAPTER III.

By the end of his first day at Mentone
John Lawrence had made up his mind that
he would leave again immediately—as soon,
in fact, as civility to Lady Mordaunt admitted of his doing so. He did not, he told
himself, like the place. It was pretty
enough in its way, still he did not like it.
It was a mere teacup with a crowd of
wretched invalids crowded together like
ants at the bottom, and a wall of rocks all
round which none of them could ever climb.
It was sheer waste of time spending any of
his fast-vanishing leave in such a spot,
when there were dozens of places infinitely
more worth visiting awaiting him further
on. No, he would not delay. Why should

he? there was nothing to detain him, he
was as free as air, and it was rather absurd
if a man could not make use of his own
freedom without consulting other people.

At the end of a week, however, he had
not gone, and by that time a certain dis-
inclination to move, which he had once or
twice before experienced, seemed to have
overtaken him. Some part of that familiar
charm which had made Mordaunt more of
a home than any place he had ever had a
right to call by that name, seemed to renew
itself under these altered circumstances.
Every morning he made up his mind that he
would start next day for Genoa, and every
night, after spending the evening at Les
Avants, he remembered, as he walked back to
his hotel, that he had forgotten to announce
that intention. Lady Helversdale had returned to England the day after her mother-
in-law's arrival, so that Lady Mordaunt
and her grand-daughter were alone at the
villa, and expected to be alone for at least
a month. After balancing the matter in

his own mind for some days, the Major all
at once, for no assignable reason, arrived
at exactly an opposite decision from his
previous one, and decided upon remaining
where he was for the present. There was
no use, he told himself, in fussing. As for
picture-galleries, even if he remained a
month—and he had no intention of staying
as long—there would be plenty of time for
them, and as for scenery, everybody knew
that there was no limit to the scenery to be
seen along the shores of the Mediterranean !

One thing he was clear about not liking,
and that was his hotel. It had filled up
rapidly since the night of his arrival, and
was more celebrated for the number of bedrooms it contained, than for the tranquillity
which it bestowed upon their inmates.
Partly at Lady Mordaunt's suggestion,
partly because the idea fitted with his own
bent for solitude, he betook himself and
his properties at the end of a week to a
couple of rooms, situated in a house half-
way up the side of the hill which rose

behind Les Avauts.   There were some five
hundred steps, more or less, to be climbed
before attaining his abode, and for this and
other reasons it had not been taken that
season, and the proprietor was willing to
let a portion of it, even upon the understanding that the tenant was free to give it
up if he choose at a day's notice.   No one
could call it a convenient situation, but the
position when attained was superb.   From
the little brown balcony which ran round
two sides of the house, and overhung the
declivity, you looked straight on to the
roofs of the houses below, and over their
crowded confusions, to the blue sweep and
splendour of the bay, the Cap Martin—
usually to Mentonese observation bounding
everything to westward—sinking into its
proper place as a long green tongue of land
with woods running seaward, washed upon
both sides by low blue waves, danced over
here and there with points of white.

Upon this balcony it became our Major's
habit to imbibe his morning cup of coffee,

and smoke his morning cigar. At the back
of the house, mounting so suddenly that a
few yards off it came to be on a level with
the upper windows, there ran a small lane,
paved with loose stones, and shut in upon
either side with a high wall, in which were
two doors, one opening into the garden of
the house he occupied, the other into
another, and larger one upon the other
side. This garden seemed to be chiefly
given up to pumpkins, lolling globose
heads along the ground, and was over-
shadowed by a couple of immense loquat
trees, while in the centre stood a small
mysterious pink house, with a solitary
aperture tightly shut in by a pair of green
discoloured *contre-vents*. It was never
apparently visited by any owner, but there
was a gardener who possessed a fine baritone voice, which could be heard sounding,
now from a tomato patch, now from a
clump of cassias or loquats, half extinguished as he stooped to ply his avocations,
but anon booming into sudden resonance

as he stood upright. This man—his name
John discovered to be Giacomo—possessed
in addition to his baritone voice a wife,
whose magnificent black eyes used to come
flashing up the lane as he appeared, carrying her husband's dinner in a striped red
pocket-handkerchief, whereupon the two
used to adjourn together to eat it in the
shadow of one of the walls.

Rather to his own astonishment the
Major developed a considerable liking for all
this. He liked to sit upon the balcony, and
watch the lizards darting hither and thither,
their vibrant tongues outstretched in search
of flies, coming nearer and nearer, until
one, more audacious than the rest, would
perhaps cross his foot, or vanish with a
crackling noise under his newspaper. It
amused him to speculate upon the ways
of Giacomo and his wife Battista, and
through them, of the other Giacomos and
Battistas; to listen, however unavailingly,
to their talk, and return a friendly nod to
their beaming salutations. He took, too,

with fresh keenness to his old pursuits, and spent a good many idle hours amongst the olive yards and upon the stony ridges of the hills, getting intimate with the ways of Mentonese ants, and authoritative as regards the habits of that socially important person the Trap-door spider, who, if aware of its own distinction, must be gratified at so notable a triumph over immemorial prejudice.

Better still he liked to get into that region of absolute stoniness which lends so peculiar a character to the hills about Mentone. It had been a surprise to him to find such possibilities of wildness, almost savagery, so near the beaten track. Warm as it continued to be in the valleys and upon the littoral, a good deal of snow had fallen up here since his arrival, and there were rock pockets and unsunned recesses full of it. Where the olives cease, and the reign of pure rock begins, these hills are crossed and recrossed with minute foot-paths, scratched rather than worn, invisible altogether in some lights, and coming out stronger in others, like wrinkles upon an ageing face. Higher still there comes a point where these, too, cease, and save at one or two places where paths have been cut and mules occasionally pass, a visitor is nearly as rare a vision as upon the sky-kissed summit of Monte Rosa or Mount Ararat.

He liked to linger in this upland region until the short afternoon had waned, and the sun was beginning to throw deep indigo-blue shadows across the fluted ridges. Then, taking the slope of the hills for a guide, he would scramble down, first over sheer rock, then across a neutral ground where green battalions of pines were yearly pushing upwards, and clinging with tenacious clutch to spots where a roothold seemed an impossibility; gradually attaining to the conquered or half-conquered portion of the slopes, where the feathery foliage of olives began to mingle with the denser spikes of the pines, and where an occasional wall, banked up with earth, told that the interminable struggle had again begun. On and on, till the sup-

porting walls grew closer, and perhaps a
white or pink-faced house, close shut and
deserted, lifted itself out of the encompassing
greenery. Then the first indications of
habitation—the bark of a dog ; a few belated
olive-pickers, lifting black astonished eyes
from their baskets to see who was passing ;
the cheery "buona sera," exchanged with
some beetle-browed woman stirring *polenta*
upon her doorstep. Then duskier still and
duskier, as the rapid southern night gathered
its pinions about him. A stony foot-path,
stumbled upon by accident ; a flock of sheep
being incited to commit trespass by its small,
hairy-coated guide ; the keen aromatic scent
of the rosemaries and junipers, strengthened
under a dash of dew; then, counteracting
these, a flavour of tobacco and garlic ;
the last steep descent ; a bridge over a
nearly waterless torrent bed ; the sudden
ear-piercing shriek of a locomotive ; and
Mentone, with its many-twinkling lights
and its hundred and one hotels, was again
around him.

After a day spent in this peripatetic fashion he would saunter up of an evening to Les Avants, and devote the time till bed-hour to Lady Mordaunt and her grand-daughter. Young Mr. Cathers, he soon discovered, seldom came at that hour. His alarm of his future grandmother-in-law was evidently not entirely a humorous pretence, and he preferred enjoying. the company of his *fiancée* at hours when he could do so without the constraint of her presence.

There was no question of an immediate marriage, so the Major, not a little to his relief, learnt. It was to be postponed at least six months, possibly a year, in consideration of the youth of the bride, and also of the health of the bridegroom, whose lungs, despite the blooming vigour of his appearance were still held to require attention.

Personally, nothing could be more civil —as with some inward irritation he could not but admit—than the young man's manner to himself. If there was anything

not exactly cordial in his own behaviour—
and he could not but suspect there must be
—the other either did not perceive it, or
had made up his mind to overcome it by
his own geniality. That the voice of the
locality was in his favour, there could be no
question. Setting aside Lady Mordaunt,
whose animosity dated, she had admitted,
from a recent period, he was unquestionably
a popular personage at Mentone. He had
established himself indeed upon a footing
not usual at his age. The amount of local
hospitality was not just then large, and of
that limited quantity a considerable propor-
tion was exercised by his mother and himself, rather by himself and his mother, for
that good lady never went the length of
ordering a cup of tea or a saucer of ice
without the concurrence of her son.

From what Lady Mordaunt had said the
Major was prepared to find them established
with some luxury, but the size of the house
took him by surprise. It would have been
a large one anywhere, and was very large

for Mentone. In style it was Italian, or pseudo-Italian, and if not unimpeachable in point of architecture, the general effect was certainly good. There were two loggias, one in a tower, the other opening out of an upstairs sitting-room, which was the special property of the young master of the house. That description might indeed apply with perfect propriety to every corner of it, for his hand was visible throughout, and if the decoration inclined to the heterogeneous— to a wild helter-skelter of all conceivable styles and colours—that, after all, is a fault for which the sun of the south has a traditionary kindness.

It was the garden of the Villa Splendide —the Cathers, to do them justice, were not responsible for the name—which constituted its chief feature, and of this garden the most important points were the palms. Of these there were a great many, four especially, which stood in sentinel fashion on each side of the house, being of exceptional height and amplitude. They had not been grown

where they stood, having been only placed
there some six or seven years earlier by the
previous proprietor, a Parisian banker, from
whom the Cathers had taken it. A palm is
a wonderfully complacent vegetable, however, and no one looking at the ribbed
splendours of their shafts, or the crowning
glories of their magnificent coronals of
fronds, would have believed in so recent a
transportation.

Naturally the Major was not long at
Mentone without renewing his acquaintance
with Mrs. Cathers. She had not altered
much since his first recollection of her.
Her contours were, perhaps, somewhat more
redundant, but to make amends, her toilettes
were decidedly less brilliant than they used
to be. It seemed to him, too, that she talked
less, and that her colloquial fluency had
sustained some corrective touches—changes
which he shrewdly suspected to be due to
the restraining hand of the all-accomplished
Algernon. To do that brilliant young man
justice, he appeared an excellent son. After

all possible prunings and tonings had been effected, good Mrs. Cathers' air, style, and conversation were scarcely what so fastidious a young gentleman could be supposed to feel proud of presenting to the world in the person of his surviving parent. No symptom, however, of so unworthy a sentiment ever, so far as the Major could observe, appeared in his manner or conversation. This may have been only a refinement of taste, but it had all the effect of good-heartedness, and as such he was ready to give him credit for it.

As regards another and an even more important point—his devotion to his *fiancée* —he was much less satisfied; perhaps it would be truer to say that, as time went on, he tried to be more dissatisfied than he really felt. He was in love—Oh yes; no doubt he was in love, but was he as much in love as he ought to be? that was the question. Had he any idea what a generous, large-hearted, exceptional nature the beneficent heavens had bestowed upon him in

the person of his future wife ? or was it only
her more obvious, as it were adventitious,
claims to consideration—youth, good looks,
rank, all that is summed up in the word
position—which attracted him? John
Lawrence's private opinion—but this, it must
be remembered, was a prejudiced one—was
that the latter was the case. He did not
believe, with all his evident intelligence,
that he was capable of anything else, and
the more he saw them together the less he
believed it.

Upon the other hand there was — unfortunately he felt—no doubt about the
girl's feelings towards her betrothed. He
believed her to be under a rapturous hal-
lucination, to be living in a silver-lined cloud
of idealization, one which being only seen
from the inside, the lining alone was visible.
She was very much in love, of that he felt
no doubt. It was first love, in its most
ardent, most impressionable, most ingenuous
form. Lady Mordaunt's theory of the matter
had evidently been based upon a misconcep-

tion. However the declaration may have
come about, he felt sure that the hero of it
had no occasion to threaten a speedy consumption in order to ensure acceptance;
on the contrary he believed that the acceptance when it came had been pronounced
with gratitude, with a rush of wondering
happiness in which head, heart, taste, all
went together in consenting union.

Let one be as prejudiced, too, as one would
—and in his secret soul our friend was conscious of being about as prejudiced as a man
could be—it was impossible to deny that
there was much about this youngster which
to a girl of seventeen must make him seem
a very fit object for idealization. Elly,
moreover, had never been wont to do things
by halves. If she liked you, she liked
everything about you, and her liking only
became the stronger under the stimulating
effect of opposition.

This essential element, which under ordinary circumstances might in this case have
been fatally wanting, was amply supplied

by the position which Lady Mordaunt had taken up, indeed, one unfortunate result of the engagement was the sort of half estrangement which it had brought between the grand-daughter and grandmother. Of her lack of appreciation of her future grandson-in-law, the latter, as we know, made very little secret. On the contrary, flaunted it in the face of all men—

"It is an odd thing," she said one day, when the door had just closed upon the lovers, and she and the Major were *tête-à-tête*—"It is an odd thing, but last year I was rather inclined, do you know, to like that young man than otherwise. He seemed less opaque, more perceptive, more anxious to make himself amiable than most of the young gentlemen of his standing. But since he has been what may be called a member of the family, though his amiability has not diminished—quite the contrary—I find myself growing hourly to hold him in greater and greater detestation. It is as much now as I can do to contain myself when he

comes into the room! It is very unfortunate, and I am aware that the fault may be
on my side, but still the fact remains. If
you could enable me to see him with different
eyes, I should be only too thankful, but
what can I do? It is to me as if he were
one of those nasty sea-creatures of yours,
which pretend to be flowers, and all the
while are horrid little beasts, with a whole
armament of nasty little stings. He seems
so essentially meretricious—as a work of
art, I mean—like an indifferent picture
copied by a fifth-rate copyist. His very
good looks have come to wear a tawdry
aspect in my eyes; the looks of a barber's
block—an extremely expensive barber's
block, I willingly grant you, but still in that
style. If you are told some fine day that I
have thrown a tea-cup at his head, you had
better make haste to contradict the report
before inquiring into the facts! As to amiability, no wonder he is amiable when he
has all the cards in his hands! He knows
that though I may snap, I have absolutely

no power; that the thing is as much fixed
and settled, I suppose, as if they were
married already. When I think of that
child Elly as his wife I really can hardly
contain myself! It is not, believe me, anything so vulgar as his want of birth, or of
his money having been made in trade. If
these come into the matter, they are mere
straws and chips. What I feel about him,
I should feel just the same if he were a
young duke. His blankets are infinitely
less distasteful to me than he is himself."

To this and many similar outpourings the
Major answered little—as little, in fact, as
he could. There seemed nothing to say,
and he had a masculine objection to kicking
his toes against the pricks of an established
fact. That he agreed with Lady Mordaunt
it is needless to observe. To him, more
even than to her, the idea of this marriage
was repugnant beyond all words. He even
went the length several times of assuring
himself that the girl were better dead than

married to that young man. And then—
with that recoil from an exaggerated antipathy which an honest mind feels—he
would ask himself what justification he had
for taking so extravagant a view of the
matter. Here, upon the one hand was a
young lady well born, but penniless—for
even her grandmother's money, which
under happier circumstances might have
come to her share, would be needed to keep
up the credit of the future head of the
house—and here, upon the other hand, was
a young man of exemplary conduct, as far
as any one could say, of agreeable manners,
irreproachable tastes, and princely, or grand
ducal fortune, who asked for nothing but
the young lady herself, without the addition
of a penny piece. Was that the sort of
suitor any one in these days could be
expected to treat with scorn ?

Of the more serious flaws which had
seemed to him observable in the boy
Cathers—a want of manliness, and a decided turn for ingenious fibbing—it is only

fair to say that, so far, he had not seen a
symptom. They appeared to have vanished
in company with his sullenness and peevish
irritability. Unquestionably he had altered
very much, so much as to amount to what
might fairly be called a transformation.
How far it was a change of nature, if there is
such a thing, or how far the more pleasing
qualities had merely overlapped the others,
time alone could show. Where the Major
did now and then catch a glimpse of what
in his own mind he called the hairy hoof,
was in a certain over-accentuation in his
tone about money. His consciousness of
his wealth seemed to be not merely chronic
—that, perhaps, was natural—but acute, as
if it was never much further from his mind
than the small change from his trousers
pocket. Another trait which seemed to
show some want of what are called the right
instincts, was a sort of nonchalant consciousness which he now and then let slip
as regard the fact of his *fiancée's* rank and
social standing, though even this was an

accusation which he felt it would be rather difficult to substantiate.

A little incident which happened one afternoon brought out these two traits it seemed to him with some distinctness.

He had gone in response to an invitation to see a picture which was in process of painting at the Villa Splendide. It was apparently part of young Cathers' taste for the decorative that he had almost always a painter, sculptor, or artist of some sort engaged in executing commissions for him. This was to be one of a set of panels, with figures representing scenes of local life, destined to fill certain niches above the mantle-piece of the owner's sitting-room.

The painter was a young Frenchman of no reputation, but considerable self-belief, who chanced to be staying at Mentone, and with whom young Cathers had made acquaintance. When the Major arrived upon the scene, the two betrothed young people and Mrs. Cathers were standing in a sort of courtyard at the back of the house, where an easel had been set up, and where the painter was busily at work. A model had been secured—the housemaid of the villa,—who stood posed in the sunshine, with a basket of flowers on her arm, a small hat much askew upon her head, and no doubt in the first instance as much of an engaging smile as could be achieved upon her face. It was to be a scene of rustic courtship, and a lover was already hovering in the distance in the person of a good-looking under-gardener, a Sardinian. The arch smile, however, had effectually by this time fled from the model's face. The poor girl was evidently tired to death, and desperately bored by the whole proceeding. She kept her head in the required position, but her eyes, wearily revolving, seemed to ask when the hour's penance would be at an end, and she might return to the welcome relaxation of housemaiding.

Of these symptoms the artist—whose pictorially - twirled moustache seemed a guarantee for his capabilities,—was evidently

unaware. He dabbled about amongst his
oil-tubes and mediums, tried effects and
effaced them again, threw in a shadow there,
and a high light here, and then stood back
to judge of the result, conscious to the full
evidently of the gallery, but not at all of the
discomfort of his victim. Elly Mordaunt
was naturally less pre-occupied.

" Poor thing, she looks dreadfully tired ! "
she said in an undertone to her lover, just
as the Major joined the group. " Don't you
think she ought to rest, Algernon ? Do tell
him so."

" Lady Eleanor declares you are wearing
out your model, M. Flarion," the young man
announced in fluent French. John Lawrence
had already had occasion to remark his
capabilities in this direction, especially in
contrast to his own manifest inability to
utter two consecutive sentences in the language. " It won't do to have her falling ill
in the middle of your picture, will it ? Tiens,
Jeannette ! here is something to comfort
your tired legs, ma fille,—" handing the girl

a coin. "Remercier miladi," he added, carelessly indicating Lady Eleanor with a gesture of one hand.

"No, no, not me! You will hurt her feelings, Algernon," she whispered reproachfully. "I think the picture will be very pretty," she went on to the girl with a blush, and in French which was neither so fluent nor so unimpeachable at his. "And very like you," she added.

"Monsieur Flarien is sure to make it *that!*" the young master of the house pronounced with an air of lordly connoisseurship. "I want him to do you, Elly—that is if Lady Mordaunt approves. Well, as Jeannette is resting herself, we may as well go and rest too. Will you come upstairs to my den? I want to exhibit some things I got the other day at Marseilles. There are a lot of weapons specially which I am dying to have a dispassionate opinion about. I know Major Lawrence is an authority upon killing tackle, and there are some inlaid things—scimitars and yatagans—which I

bought of a Jew, and which he told me came
from Fez, but which ever since I have had
a dreadful suspicion are merely Birming-
ham or Sheffield bewitched. Will you tell
them to bring tea there, mother? It is
early still, but Elly has had a walk, and
we should all feel the better for it. For
my part, I am a Russian in my powers of
tea-drinking."

They had their tea, and the scimitars and
yatagans were duly inspected, their pur-
chaser declaring that he knew that he had
been grotesquely imposed upon, but that
the old fellow was so diabolically plausible,
and anything Oriental had such a fascina-
tion for him, that he could never help his
desire for possession from appearing in his
face, with the inevitable result of sending
prices sky-high in a twinkling.

Suddenly he interrupted himself in the
midst of his disquisition to declare that they
were wasting the afternoon, they must come
out again into the garden and see the
yuccas, three of which he had discovered

that morning to be in full blossom. Elly and the Major must see them at once.

They adjourned accordingly into the garden. Here, as was natural, the lovers were presently discovered to have strayed away down a bye-path, presumably in search of the yuccas, leaving the Major to the entertainment of Mrs. Cathers.

He had no dislike for that amiable lady, quite the contrary. There was even a certain mild amusement to be found in her evident struggles to keep watch over her colloquial infirmities, and in all things to recall what was required of her by the higher powers. It was absolutely impossible for her to converse upon any earthly subject, however, except one, namely, "the goodness, brightness, majesty, and glory of the King" —her king, that prince and flower of young men, her son Algernon. Algernon's tastes, Algernon's extraordinary gift for languages, Algernon's paintings, Algernon's intentions for the future, Algernon's interest in flowers and his capability for remembering their dreadful Latin names, which all sounded to *her* alike ; Algernon's return of cough this winter, and her anxieties in consequence.

"It's from my side of the family, he gets it, and that's the worst," she observed self-reproachfully. "My eldest brother had two daughters die of consumption, the second was a beautiful girl, just turned eighteen, she had been proposed to the year before by a baronet."

The Major expressed suitable commiseration.

"Yes, indeed it was very hard upon poor Joseph, wasn't it ? Thank God, Algernon's isn't like that, only he has to be very careful. Indeed, he generally is, that I will say. There never was a better son in *this* world than Algernon!" She paused as if lost in the contemplation of his filial virtues, then resumed.—

"And to think of his going to be married ! I declare I can't get used to it, and that's the truth ! Not but what if he was to marry there's any one I'd choose sooner than Lady

Elly—I suppose I ought to say Elly, only somehow I can't get my tongue round it. She is a dear girl, no pride or nonsense about her, no more than if she was nobody, and Lady Mordaunt too—so clever and agreeable, wonderfully clever, isn't she?— Lady Mordaunt, I mean. Some people say *too* clever, but I never thought so myself, we always got on ever since I first came to the country, so it don't seem like strangers. Of course, it's very dreadful about the Earl. Poor man, what a way he does seem to have been going on! All that horse-racing! I'm sure if I was Lady Helversdale I'd never have an easy moment. So sad for the family, too. Not that it matters so much for girls. Nobody would expect Lady Elly to take to horse-racing because her poor papa did, though, indeed, people *do* say that sort of thing is getting dreadful common amongst the aristocracy, ladies as well as gentlemen. I can't say myself, for I haven't been, not in regular society since I was a girl, there are always terrible stories in the newspapers, but one never knows whether they are true or not, they must be putting something in to fill themselves out, mustn't they? My father belonged to the Wesleyan persuasion, and we were all brought up very strict. I was only once at a dance before I was married, and then I wasn't let dance. It was at a Mrs. Mellars or Medlars—I can't quite think of the name, though I know it began with an M.—they lived in Russell Street, close to Russell Square. It was a big house with a porch to the door, and the servant that opened it had on knee-breeches and white stockings, I remember. It was the first time I'd ever seen such a thing, and I thought he must have forgotten his other clothes!"

Mrs. Cathers sighed gently, then, after this momentary diversion, reverted to Algernon and his plans, and all the things he intended to do once he came of age, and how thankful she herself would be when that happened. "Not that there had

been anything really to complain of in
the trustees, still a young man—a spirited
young man, you know, like Algernon —
likes to feel free to dispose of his own
money without consulting any one, as is
only right and proper, seeing that it *is* his
own."

It was not the most congenial of subjects
to the Major, still he had too much kindliness to do otherwise than listen with due
attentiveness to the good lady's outpourings.
The edges of the walks were wet, and he
observed that every now and then Mrs.
Cathers made a violent clutch at her
garments, which seemed heavier and
warmer than the season, or at any rate
the warmth of the weather called for.
This attracted his attention to them, which
otherwise he might have passed without
notice, and having done so, he discovered
here, too, traces of that filial tyranny under
which she lived, moved, and had her being.
That her costume was the result of her
son's views of feminine attire was evident

at a glance. It was of some heavy silken material, of dark olive shading into a black, and fell over her ample figure in sculpturesque folds which would have done honour to a Roman matron. Unfortunately for the general effect in her hasty exit from the house she had snatched up a sun-bonnet, lined with magenta sarcenet, and crowned with a wreath of blue and pink flowers, below which, her amiable countenance glowed with a double glow, that of the sun and the reflection of the magenta lining.

Having twice made the entire circuit of the garden, they paused at last upon the summit of a small detached eminence, approached by a succession of wide shallow steps, chipped out of the rock. Below extended a length of pergola, supported upon square pillars of loosely piled stones, and overgrown with a crowd of variegated creepers, red, purple, yellow — a perfect kaleidoscope of tints.

Mrs. Cathers seated herself upon a knoll, and wiped her forehead, tilting her sun-

bonnet backwards for the purpose. The
Major set his back against a rock, pulled
his moustache, and meditated effecting his
escape. A couple of green fly-catchers
came darting by with a rapid " click, click "
of small brown bills, returning to a twig
between whiles, and panting vehemently
from their exertions. Presently there arose
a whispering sound of rustling boughs immediately below them, and, looking over
into the bosky depths beneath, they saw
the two lovers — their heads, rather, for
everything below the shoulders was hidden
beneath the cloud of greenery.

They were walking slowly along, engaged
in earnest talk. Every now and then
Algernon Cathers would hold back some
long trailing bough, under which Elly would
pass with her head slightly bent, then he
would let it go, and the verdure would close
in again with the same whispering noise
upon their track. It was like the passage
of some nymph and demi-god in the far-
back youth of the world; the dark supple

beauty of the one, the tall maidenly vigour
and stateliness of the other, telling admirably
as a composition.   John Lawrence started.
What there was new or unexpected about
the vision he would have been puzzled to
say, and yet it seemed to him somehow
quite new and very startling indeed.   It
was almost as if it was the first time he had
seen them together.   His hand tightened
unconsciously over a fragment of orange-
blossom he happened to be holding, and an
odd angry light came into his eyes.

For a moment the garden and everything
around seemed to whirl and dance fantastic-
ally.   A sudden sensation of scorching came
over him; a wrath which seemed to break
in waves across his breast.   He felt carried
out of himself, carried almost out of his
own control, by the sight and all that it
suggested.   An impulse came over him—
a perfectly insane impulse—an impulse then
and there to spring down that broken
flowery slope, and to rush between them;
to thrust them apart, if need be by main

force. It seemed as if now, only now he had realized that they were pledged; that henceforth they were one, not two; that she—Elly Mordaunt—belonged, absolutely *belonged* to that young man—that insinuating, black-eyed young man whom he himself could crush with one hand as easily as he could a kitten. His hand clenched instinctively at the thought; his mouth set; all the lines of his face seemed suddenly to have grown older, harder, more accentuated. The mildest usually of men, he looked suddenly dangerous.

Mrs. Cathers, too, looked into the green abyss with a dissatisfied air. The sources of her dissatisfaction were, however, different.

"Deary me I do wish Algernon wouldn't go routing about amongst all those moist plants!" she said fretfully. "I'd like to call and beg him to come up and anyhow to put his hat on, do look at him, walking about with it in his hand! I'm afraid, though, he might be vexed. Maybe they don't know we can see them from here, and it might look like spying on them, mightn't it now?"—addressing her companion appealingly.

But John Lawrence answered never a word. He could not. He was fighting a battle; one which required all the strength he possessed. Mrs. Cathers took his silence apparently as a sign of agreement.

"Ah well maybe we *had* better leave them alone," she said, reseating herself with an air of resignation. "He can't get much harm so long as he don't sit down, and I hope Lady Elly would have sense enough to prevent *that*. She'll have to learn to do so if they're going to be married, so she may as well begin at once. It is natural, after all, he should like getting her away by himself, isn't it?" she continued, a tender motherly smile curving her kind stout face. "Young men will be young men, and all young men like doing their courting by themselves. You know all about that, I'll be bound, Major, though you do make yourself out so wonderful old and wise ! You can't expect them to be *always* thinking of their healths, can you ? Nobody can ever be young more than once in *this* life, and that's the truth ! " the good lady ended, with a sigh.

CHAPTER IV.

The unprecedented amiability of the
weather that season at Mentone was a
source of much congratulation to all the
little colony gathered about the feet of St.
Agnese and her rock-crowned sisters. Day
after day the sun got up in a business-like
fashion, swept the whole arc of sky without
a moment's diminution of its splendour, and
returned to bed with the same sort of
matter-of-course magnificence with which it
had arisen. It seemed as if the weather
was wound up, and could not change for
the worse, even if it tried. Socially, on the
other hand, the season was not so well
spoken of. The greater number of the
villas were unlet, although the hotels it was

said were crammed. The Major, not being an *habitué*, was not of course qualified to form an opinion, not to say that the fewer people the better he would have been contented. There was a considerable muster, he observed, of chairs at Les Avants whenever he happened to drop in there of an afternoon, either in the little salon, or upon the little terrace outside, which latter, being covered with an awning, answered practically all the purposes of a verandah.

It was rather a surprise to him to discover how shy Elly Mordaunt often was upon these not very formidable social occasions. She dispensed the tea and did her duty in catering for the afternoon appetites of her grandmother's guests, but it was evident that she did it as a duty merely, and it was rarely that her voice was heard mingling with those of the other tea-drinkers.

How far this was due to the strained relations existing between her and her grandmother, it was difficult for him to tell, not having seen her previously. Personally he could not complain, for it had the effect of throwing them a good deal together, both being, as it were, outside the regular Mentonese set, as well as outside that passing world of travellers — celebrities many of them of a generation back—who lingered to pay a passing tribute to Lady Mordaunt. When no tea was in question they used to saunter together round the little garden, straying often thence into the olive yards or along the small steep walk which led from the gate of Les Avants to the beach and esplanade below. In this way they took up their old friendship again pretty much where it had been left off, the broken links renewing themselves naturally as the old habit of intercourse re-asserted itself.

Unconsciously, rather than consciously, Elly let him see a good deal of her own life, its thoughts, fancies, pursuits, stopping short, however, of its most recent development. He could not, at times, help a certain amount of half-humorous mortifica-

tion at the serene perception of his immense
age which she evidently possessed, and
which gave its tone to everything she said.
No doubt to the eye of seventeen he was
a hoary veteran, a being of vast age and
experience. For all that, he was, as a
matter of fact, it must be remembered,
barely thirty-eight, and at thirty-eight a
man has a perfect right to consider himself
a young man still if he chooses—as much
right, many people would say, as a dozen
years earlier.

Even Lady Mordaunt, to whom the difference between twenty-eight and thirty-
eight would, under ordinary circumstances,
have been imperceptible, took — perhaps
from habit—much the same view of the
matter. More than once, when there was
question of some expedition to which she
declined to let Elly go escorted only by
her lover, the objection was instantly withdrawn when it was understood that Major
Lawrence had consented to be of the party.
Young Cathers, too, showed not the smallest

symptom of jealousy, a circumstance which
the elder man felt in some doubt whether
to put down to the debtor or creditor side
of that account which he mentally kept
open against that fortunate young gentleman's name!

Long afterwards, in lonely moments, in
interminable Indian days when the great
heat made everything seem unreal and
ghostly, on breathless nights when he lay
broad awake listening to the recurrent
sweeping of his punkah, those half-hours
under the vaporish olives, or beside the
peacock-tinted Mediterranean, came back
to the poor Major's mind with a vividness
greater even than they possessed at the
time. He could see Elly Mordaunt's grey
eyes—eyes which seemed to grow lighter
and darker from moment to moment, as
some grey eyes do—her tall, alert young
figure; the pure, somewhat severe lines of
her profile, set in its masses of brown hair.
He was not a particularly imaginative
man, yet there was something about the

girl's whole image which seemed always
to suggest curious thoughts—thoughts of
spring mornings, of wide unbroken pros-
pects, of everything large, simple, untram-
melled; everything that was furthest re-
moved from what was narrow, tortuous,
conventional.

Despite her eyes, Elly Mordaunt was not
by any means a recognized beauty at that
time, though she came to be spoken of
as one in later days. She was not even
accounted "winning" or "taking," gave herself, indeed, little trouble to win the suffrages
of her neighbours. It seemed as if her life
had got into a waiting stage, as if she
were walking about in a sort of suspense,
expecting something, something that had
not yet revealed itself. As a result of this
indifference and dreaminess, she was not
particularly popular, indeed, there were not
a few people ready to wonder what young
Mr. Cathers—such a delightful young man,
and so clever—could see in *that* Lady
Eleanor Mordaunt, such a dull girl, and

not pretty even—oh, dear no, gawky and stiff, and so *much* too tall !

John Lawrence lost himself in speculations as to her precise attitude of mind with regard to her beautiful lover, but he had only his speculations for his pains, for she never spoke upon the subject, avoiding with a sort of fierce maidenliness even remote and merely general references to it.

When at rest her face generally expressed a kind of sober contentedness, no great outward exuberance, but a steady flood of happiness welling upwards as if from invisible sources. It filled the looker-on with pity, with sudden rushes of sympathy, with fierce irritation, all at once. Had she *no* doubts then ? he used to ask himself, as he trudged up his twice two hundred steps of an evening, on his way back from Les Avants. Was she putting her life in absolute blind unhesitating faith into the hands of that—*that* young man ? He never got nearer towards defining the owner of the Villa Splendide than this blank formula, the robustness of his prejudice not requiring, perhaps, any stimulus to flog it into greater violence.

Some evenings he abstained from going to Les Avants at all. He felt as if it was impossible to meet those trust-filled eyes without saying something; without thrusting upon her, however ineffectually, some warning; without imploring her to pause, before hazarding her all upon such a venture. How—knowing young Cathers as she had known him formerly—*could* she trust him so implicitly? he would ask himself with an ever-increasing astonishment.

It touched him by moments intensely, this confidence of hers, and yet it hurt him, hurt him as he had never in all his life been hurt by anything before. Soberest and least demonstrative of men, he grew quite rampant—it was always when he was safely by himself—over the thought of those perils she was fronting so lightly. He appealed to her again and again in the most moving terms—when she was not there—to pause,

not to rush so heedlessly upon her ruin.
"Child, are you mad? have you no eyes?
Look! Think! Remember!" he would
exclaim to the vacant air. Never having
had anything to spare in the matter of
comeliness, the poor Major grew even
leaner and grimmer than usual as he
brooded over all this. He rambled in its
company amongst the peaks over-topping
his lodgings, and he watched it amongst
the sparkling ripples of the bay beneath.
If by moments he forgot it, it came back
with an ugly rush like the remembrance of
some approaching catastrophe. Again and
again he upbraided himself with his own
supineness, his own ox-like torpor. Yet
what could he do? What excuse had he—
a stranger—for interfering, when even Lady
Mordaunt—who made no secret of her
detestation to the engagement—contented
herself with that negative condemnation;
when every other relation the girl possessed
in the world regarded it with hilarious
satisfaction; when it was known to be the

one subject which Lord and Lady Helversdale had been agreed upon for years?

He felt often sorry in those days for his
kind old friend. Like many people, Lady
Mordaunt was a little bit the victim of her
own *rôle*. Her imperious ways, her grand
air, her little sharp speeches, imposed upon
others, imposed also to some extent upon
herself. People heard them, but they did
not see what lay behind them, and to which
they were the mere screen and outer en-
trenchment. They did not see that there
was a very tender, often a very lonely heart
behind; a heart which craved for something
which it very rarely got. She was a *grande
dame*, but she was a tender-hearted old
woman too, as no one knew better, few as
well as John Lawrence himself. It seemed
to him that Elly showed just a little hard-
ness, a little want of tenderness, and even
gratitude towards her grandmother. How
far there had been any real confidence
between them before Algernon Cathers
began to loom large upon the scene he

could not know, but it was clear that this confidence, if it had ever existed, had for the moment dried up; that the girl resented the poor estimation in which her beautiful lover was held, while the elder woman's pride forbade her to press for a reconciliation.

Sometimes he used to see Lady Mordaunt give a quick glance to where Elly would sit in a sort of open-eyed trance, her grey eyes fixed on space, her hands hanging listlessly at her side. After this momentary glance the grandmother would look away again, sometimes with an angry jerk, sometimes with a short sharp sigh, stifled in the utterance. She was more imperious than ever in those days, more sharp-tongued too, and autocratic, snubbing her visitors, French as well as English, with remorseless vigour. Indeed, there was a certain much-decorated vicomte, a devoted and lifelong admirer of hers, who was so persistently maltreated one afternoon, that the Major met him coming away afterwards in the garden, as he believed, in tears!

So matters went on, and one week slid
into the next, and the weather broke and
mended again, and the usual busy idle
routine of the place went on. Since
nothing remains absolutely the same, so
now there was a slow but unmistakable
change, and that change was in John
Lawrence himself. He was aware of it,
and yet not aware. He was not a man
given to dwelling upon his own symptoms,
to laying his finger physically or senti-
mentally upon his own pulse, and such a
man may go on for a long time before he
discovers his ailment, nay, even after
discovering it, may ignore it. It was no
new revelation to him that he was very
fond of Elly Mordaunt. Had he not always
been very fond of her? Even after the
scene in the Cathers' garden, it took a long
time to convince him that his interest was
radically different to what it had been five
years earlier, and after that a considerable
time to make it clear that the difference
was of sufficient importance to matter.

Englishmen are a slow race, and John Lawrence was even typically Britannic in such matters. The revelation, like most other revelations, came, however, at last.

One morning it was proposed that the two young people, accompanied by himself, should eat an early luncheon upon some rocks on the further side of the Cap St. Martin, commanding a sweep of both lines of shore, each rivalling the other just then in colour and sparkle. A carriage was taken to the end of the point, which was as far as it could go, and, followed by a servant carrying the luncheon-basket, the three betook themselves along a narrow walk which winds above the sea, between grey bleached rocks and a grey-green flutter of cistus and rosemary.

Elly was in unusual spirits, laughing and scrambling over the crags as she used to do when she was a child. It was almost the first time John Lawrence had seen her so, for though her moods were variable, they were all wont to incline to the side of sobriety. Algernon Cathers, too, was an image of radiancy, but this in him was no variety.

They had eaten their luncheon, and the basket had been duly carried back to the carriage, when it was proposed that they would walk home, following the undulations of the shore. Algernon Cathers at first demurred. The sun was hot, and he was not at all fond of the exercise, still for so short a distance, and with so undeniable an inducement, he was ready, he at last said heroically, to make the effort. When he flagged, Elly, he felt sure, would lend an arm to support his feebleness!

Upon arriving at the beginning of the esplanade, they sat down to watch the passers-by, who circulated up and down, some briskly, others listlessly, dragging weary limbs and gazing dully at the sea, as if nauseated of its blue; others, again, wearing that air of superabundant, almost apologetic vitality, which makes the possession of rude health seem less of an undeniable advantage in such places than elsewhere.

Amongst the crowd there presently passed a young man, who nodded with an air of familiarity to Algernon Cathers, and took off his hat ceremoniously to Lady Eleanor, who upon her side responded with the slightest and stiffest of inclinations. He was not a particularly pleasing young man. His complexion was sickly, his hat, as he replaced it on his head, had a rakish air, and his mouth a cynical twist.

"That was that horrid Mr. Davenport, wasn't it?" she said to her lover, after he had gone by. "I hope he won't pass us again; I can't bear him."

"Poor being! What has he done to merit your displeasure?" he asked, in a tone of mock commiseration.

"He has done nothing, of course, at least, nothing that I know of. Only I don't like him. I don't mean to know him. He has very disagreeable eyes. I wish you didn't know him."

"He happens to be a particular friend of mine."

"Oh, don't say that, Algernon, please don't! You know you only say it to tease me. Everybody says he is not nice. He has called ever so many times at Les Avants, but grandmamma never will allow him to be shown in."

"Your dear grandmamma is not so particularly fond of me if it comes to that."

Before she could make any reply, Mr. Davenport had returned along the esplanade. This time he passed at the back of the bench they were sitting on, and as he did so touched Algernon Cathers lightly upon the arm, who immediately sprang up and followed him a few paces along the esplanade.

He came back rather hurriedly.

"Pity me," he said to Elly in a tone of self-commiseration, with a tender lover-like glance of his beautiful eyes.

"For what?" she asked.

" For the worst of reasons. I have to leave you."

" To leave us! Why ? "

"I must! Nothing short of obligation, you may be sure, would take me."

" Who obliges you? Is it that Mr. Davenport ? "

" No, no! "

" Who then ? "

" Some one who wants to see me."

" Who wants to see you in such a hurry ? "

" Well, it's a little matter of business! "

His expression, which had been slightly embarrassed, suddenly cleared, and regained its usual brilliantly ingenuous aspect. "The fact is—I didn't mention it, because it didn't seem fair, but as you insist—you remember the Lee-Warrens, who had that big villa near the Cap last year! Fred Lee-Warren, the second son, was rather a friend of mine, and seems to have got himself into a thorough scrape at Monte Carlo. Davenport brought me a message from him. He implores me to go over,

and for the love of Heaven bring him
some money; he is in pawn, it seems, to
his hotel people, and can't get away. A
regular Monte Carlo message—the sort of
thing you might put into a tract! I only
hope he won't have put a pistol to his head
before I can get there, he seems perfectly
capable of it ! "

" Oh, of course, then, go, Algernon! Of
course you are right. Poor man, how
dreadful! Pray go quickly, and take
plenty of money, don't delay, or you
may miss your train ; Major Lawrence will
walk back with me." And she almost
pushed him away.

He went, catching up his friend at the
corner of the esplanade, and hurrying with
him in the direction of the railway. A
momentary doubt stole over John Lawrence's
mind as to whether there could be anything
behind this sudden mission of benevolence.
The next minute he felt rather ashamed of
his own suspicions. Young men frequently,
it is true, tell fibs about Monte Carlo, but

they rarely pretend to be going there when
in reality they are going somewhere else!

The argument seemed conclusive, and
yet! — He turned and looked at Elly,
wondering whether any shadow of suspicion
had alighted upon her also. She was still
standing in the same place, and looking in
the direction in which Algernon Cathers
had disappeared in company with his rather
sinister friend. A faint smile sat on her
lips, her eyes had the peculiarly gleaming
light in them which they always wore when
anything stirring or adventurous was said
in her hearing. Evidently she was following her beautiful lover in imagination;
seeing him arrive at Monte Carlo; sharing
in that flush of gratified generosity with
which he relieved his impecunious friend's
necessities! John Lawrence felt indescri-
bably irritated. By a common, if also a
totally illogical process, it doubled his own
suspicions. He felt certain now that that
young man was up to some mischief.
What was he up to, though? That was
the question!

CHAPTER V.

THE walk back to Les Avants led through the principal street of Mentone, brimming over at that hour with carriages and foot-passengers. The sun was warm, the air cool, not cold but *frappé;* it seemed to tingle through the lungs and set the blood flowing in a gay response. The polyglot clatter was deafening; the market-place, as they passed it, looked as if basketfuls of shells, mixed with fish, broken pottery, and untidy rags and tags of clothing, had all been recently turned topsy-turvy upon the ground. Elly seemed a little depressed for a few minutes after her beautiful betrothed's departure, but regained her spirits as they emerged upon the bay, and rounding the

corner of the little quay, strolled along its
curving edge, flooded to the brim with its
monotonously blue flood, and dotted at this
point with crafts of various sizes and various
degrees of unseaworthiness. Presently they
halted by simultaneous impulse at a point
where the rounded symmetry was broken by
a few large boulders, crusted with pink
corallines and grey serpulæ, upon which
the sapphire-coloured curves were sketching
a reticulated pattern of dainty yellow
tracery.

The girl stepped lightly down on to one
of these loose boulders, and stood poised
there, balancing herself, and looking over
the edge into the broken prism made by the
waters, her glance following the lines of
light as they chased one another in an
endless procession. A glad young figure,
it looked, framed and half-absorbed into the
glad gay landscape. John Lawrence's eyes
rested upon it very wistfully.

"Do you know what these rocks remind
me of?" she asked, suddenly turning round

and looking up at him. "I don't know why, but just then there jumped into my head a remembrance of that first day, or evening rather, I arrived at Mordaunt, when I ran away so wickedly from poor Matty, and you came and caught me and brought me back. Do you remember?"

"Yes, I remember perfectly," he answered.

" I always believe you saved my life. I always believe I should have been drowned then if you had not come when you did."

"I hope you would," he answered, smiling.

" You hope I would? You hope that I would have been drowned?"

"As you were not it may be permitted to hope that it was my coming that prevented you."

" Ah, I see!"

She stood a moment longer upon her boulder, smiling and looking into the blueness, crisped into wide curves against the edges of the rocks, and stained here and there with pale wine-coloured tints, where seaweeds or meandering sprays of zostera gave their own colour to its limpidity. Then she sprang back and stood beside him.

"What a troublesome little wretch I was, wasn't I?" she said brightly. "And how good every one was to me—every one at Mordaunt, I mean. You particularly, Major Lawrence!" she added, resting her eyes full upon him with a frank clear look of confidence, that look which so charmed and so wounded him, poor fellow! which told so clearly the terms upon which they stood, that liking which, even under the most favourable of circumstances, would never, he told himself, have been anything but liking.

"Children are such ridiculous creatures," she went on seriously, "and I think I must have been more ridiculous than most children. I know that in those days I had the wildest dreams—wide-awake dreams, I mean—the strangest, the most impossible. I wonder if all children, or most children have the same? Do you suppose they have?"

" What sort of dreams?" he asked.

" Oh, of the great things I was going to do ; that were going to happen to me. I used to lie awake at night planning it all out and settling what I intended to do when I was grown up. It seemed so simple, so unquestionable — as if I had nothing to do but to stretch out my hand and it was done. People to be rescued—how, when, or from what, I did not know—but that was a great idea of mine. For years and years I thought of it every night of my life, and planned it all out."

" I remember your saying something of the sort once," he answered, smiling at the recollection.

" Oh, and that was only one of dozens and dozens of schemes—things I was to do ; dragons to slay ; people to set free ; injustices to find out and set right. I cannot tell you what ridiculous ideas I had. I grow hot sometimes myself now when I think of them."

"You don't feel as if you were on your way to realize any of them?" he inquired rather drily.

She looked up at him quickly, a sudden change of expression, a glance of swift displeasure awakening in her eyes. What he had said might have passed as a joke, or as meaning nothing in particular, but for a faint undercurrent of bitterness, which had pierced through, unconsciously perhaps to himself, and which sent her thoughts instantly into a new and totally different channel to that which they had been following. She did not answer for a moment; when she did, it was in a tone of sudden gravity.

"Major Lawrence—" she stopped— "Major Lawrence, you—you don't like Algernon?"

"Lady Eleanor!" He turned, startled, almost dismayed by the unexpectedness of the attack.

"I know you don't. You have never said so, but I know it. You have looked it. I have seen it in your eyes *often*."

"I am sorry my eyes should have behaved so badly," he replied, trying to pass the subject lightly off.

"If it were any one else—if it were not such a very, very old friend—I should not mind, of course," she went on, without heeding. "But you and grandmamma"— she paused, and her breath came short and fast, as it used to do when she was a child —"how am I to *help* minding what you two think?" she burst out passionately. "I have never said anything, but, of course, I have seen it, and so has *he.* We should have been blind not to do so!" She paused again, as if to give him time to speak, but he was silent—dead silent.

"It is very wrong, and unfair—*most* unfair! It is the injustice that hurts me," she went on, her eyes kindling with all their old angry light. "You ought to be ashamed of yourself, and so ought grandmamma! You take up every little foolish thing he did or said when he was a boy, and you remember it against him now. You

judge him as if he was the same now as
then. Is that just?—is that right? How
would *you* like to have all the things which
you did when you were a boy raked up and
remembered against you?" she inquired,
fronting him superbly, her whole face alight
with anger.

"Not at all, I must confess," he answered
meekly.

"Very well then why do you do it?
Why are you so—so—I don't like to say it,
but it is—mean and ungenerous? Is he
not kind and good and unselfish *now?*
Look how he has gone off, all in an instant,
to a place he particularly detests, just
because some one—not a great friend, but
a man he knew—asked him to come and
help him. And he is *always* doing things
like that—always. There is no need for me
to say it, for every one acknowledges it—
every one, that is, except you and grandmamma. He has hundreds and hundreds
of friends—nobody has so many. I cannot
think how he came to care for me, when he

has—when—I mean—when he is so much
better—brighter—everything—than I am."

"You can't expect your friends to agree
with you there," the Major answered.

"Then they *should* believe it when I tell
them," she retorted, stamping her foot with
the old childish gesture he remembered so
well. "Mustn't I know better than anybody
else what he really is? He has the most
beautiful thoughts, the most beautiful
feelings; there is no one in the world like
him—no one!"

"There are few handsomer, at any rate."

"That has nothing to do with it!" she
exclaimed angrily. "I am not speaking of
his looks. You only say that to vex me!
You all talk of his looks, as if *that* was the
chief thing! Can he help his looks?"

"Does he wish to help them?"

"I don't know whether he does or not.
I wish it. I often wish he was as ugly as
—as——"

"As myself, say."

"Oh no, much—much uglier—downright

ugly. You are not ugly at all; you only
say that, too, to vex me. You are not one
bit nice or kind as you used to be, Major
Lawrence. I used to think that there was
no one like you. When you went to India
I cried till I made myself ill. I used to
wake at night and sob and sob, because you
were gone, and I couldn't go and talk to
you. I hated the sea because it had taken
you away from us. I hated every one
and everything; I wouldn't speak even to
Algernon, when he came over to ride with
me. It seems strange, but I don't think
I liked him much in those days. It was
not until—until——" So far she had been
speaking as she would have done when she
was twelve years old, in just the same child-
like, straightforward tone of narrative. At
this point, however, she hesitated, and a
shade of deeper colour began to flit over her
face. She went on, however, after a minute,
but more shyly, turning her head a little
away as she spoke—

"Until I came to know him better. I

found that what I had taken for coldness
and, and—conceit, was really only sensi-
tiveness. He is very sensitive — *very*.
When he is with people who are not
sympathetic, who do not appreciate him,
he cannot get on, he is miserable. When
he was a boy he always felt that people
were looking down upon him and his
mother, and we at Mordaunt particularly.
That was what made him so shy and—
different when he came to see us. He
knew, of course, that though she—Mrs.
Cathers—is so kind and good, she is not—
well—not like grandmamma, for instance;
that some people might even call her vulgar.
He is devoted to his mother, but he sees it
all the same."

"He seems, indeed, an excellent son," the
Major said, honestly glad of some one point
of praise which he could cordially re-echo.

"Of course," she answered impatiently.
"And yet he knows that she was not—not
always judicious about him when he was
younger. Not going to school—that, I

suppose, could not be helped, but it was a
dreadful disadvantage. Never seeing anything of other boys; always being by himself, or with grown-up people; it is so
difficult for a boy who is brought up like
that to be really manly—to help thinking
too much of himself and his own pursuits—
being what people call spoilt. It was not
until he came abroad and made friends of
his own, and found his own place amongst
them, that he got over those disadvantages,
that he grew bright and happy and spirited,
as he is now, that he learnt to throw off his
shyness."

"He certainly does not seem to be at all
shy now."

She looked up with a fresh flush of
anger, though this time he was not aware
of having thrown any undue emphasis into
the words.

"You are most unkind! You are very,
very unfair! You are horribly unjust! I
wonder why I speak to you at all!" she
cried passionately.

"Don't say that; please don't, Lady Elly!" he said entreatingly. "Believe me, I am not as unjust as you fancy. If I do not think that he is—well, quite worthy of you, that is not saying that he has not a thousand delightful qualities; that he is not brilliant, handsome, clever, accomplished, generous—everything that a middle-aged fogey like myself finds enviable."

"Worthy of *me!*" she exclaimed superbly. "Of me! He is worthy of something much, much better, let me tell you, than me!"

"I hope at least that he does not think so himself?"

"No, he does not. But that is because he is too noble and highminded to think it! He might if he chose. It would be very natural!"

John Lawrence made no response to this assertion, but his look presumably spoke a less reverential belief in Algernon Cathers' nobility, for Lady Eleanor turned suddenly away, and walked on with her head in the air, nor did she vouchsafe another syllable until they were well within the precincts of Les Avants.

Half-way up the steep ascent she again, however, paused, and turned to him with a certain air of solemnity, the air of one who would not willingly abandon even the most hardened criminal to the error of his ways without another appeal to his better feelings.

" Major Lawrence, I know you like me— at least you used to like me when I was a little girl, and I hope you do so still now that I am big ? " She waited, as if expecting him to say something, but he was silent, and after a moment's pause she went on. "And, therefore, because I think you like me, and because I know that I like you very, very much, because you have always been one of my kindest friends ; because when I look back to it that first year I was at Mordaunt—when you used to let me run about with you—stands out as one of the happiest of my whole life—because of all this I want you to *promise* me to—to get

over this—this foolish prejudice of yours.
I ought, I know, to be too proud to take
any notice, and so I should be if it was
any one else, but I can't *bear* that *you*
should misjudge him.   He doesn't misjudge you, he likes and respects you very
much, in spite of knowing you don't care
for him.   I know that it is just a prejudice,
and that you would get over it if you saw
more of him, but you are going away, so
that there is not much time, and I want
you to promise that you will do so now at
once.   Not, you understand, for *his* sake,"
she added, with the same little lofty gesture ;
" but for mine.   Will you?   Will you?
Will you? " she continued, stretching out
both hands and seizing his insistently, holding him at the same time with her eyes,
as if to appeal, whether he would or no, to
his better self ; to induce him to fling aside
all unworthy prejudices, born of ignorance
and darkness, and to recognize the true
light shining before him in all its effulgence.

What could he do, poor fellow !   He told

her grimly that he would try, that he would
do his best, and he went away five minutes
later hating that young man Algernon
Cathers from the very bottom of his soul,
with an intensity of hatred which six
months, nay a single fortnight ago, he
would hardly have believed himself to have
been capable!

CHAPTER VI.

Turning out of the garden of Les Avants he strode back along the esplanade and up one of the side paths which led by a series of broken flights of steps to the olive slopes above.

As he mounted his steps grew quicker and quicker, until it seemed to himself as if he literally flew; as if he were seeking to escape; as if there were something behind that he was bound to fly from. An over-mastering impulse was upon him all the time to turn back, to recant his promise, to shout aloud some of those injurious epithets which seemed to be throttling him, which jostled against one another in his brain. From comparative passiveness,

his hatred of Algernon Cathers had suddenly
sprung into full activity. He clenched his
teeth in the extremity of his anger and unavailing misery. Passing up that sunny
rocky way his whole soul felt on fire. In
the depth of his perturbed soul he found
himself crying aloud those warnings, uttering
the denunciations which he had not found
the courage or the brutality to utter under
the ægis of those trust-filled eyes. " He is
a snob! He is a cur! He is a heartless,
insolent young beast! " he cried to himself.
" A small-souled, narrow-hearted egotist;
cold-blooded! cowardly! treacherous! He
is utterly unworthy of you; utterly unworthy of any noble-hearted girl. He will
make you wretched, wretched! Can you
not see it! Oh, child, be warned! Have
pity on yourself! Save yourself while
there is still time ! "

How much or how little of these unpleasant things he had any justification
for, how much he even absolutely believed,
he was not quite sure, but after that promise

which had been extorted from him, after the
silence of the last four or five weeks, there
was an untold relief in repeating them over
and over to himself; in dinning them, as it
were, into his own ears, seeing that he was
debarred by honour from dinning them
into another's. There was yet another
advantage, that it seemed to offer a
sufficient reason for detesting this engagement apart from any more personal grounds,
grounds which he still shrank from avowing
even to himself. If this young man was
half, nay, quarter of all this, surely that was
reason enough for any friend of hers desiring
at all hazards to detach her from him. He
was resolved to keep that other motive in
the background; to deny it strenuously to
himself, as he would have denied it to any
one who had been bold enough to tax him
with it. Was he not her friend? was not
that enough? what need of searching any
deeper for a feeling which ought to animate
the breast of any one who cared for her
even in the slightest, most casual degree?

He was still climbing the hill as if in the direction of his lodgings. Before arriving there, however, he turned aside to the left along the edge of a dry torrent bed, and then up another flight of steps alternating with a steep stony pathway. He had set his mind upon attaining to a particular clump of pines which lay half-way up one of the lower slopes, and would not allow himself to halt or turn aside until he had done so. At last the spot was attained, and he flung himself at full length upon the grey-green moss-covered ground, putting up his hands as a pillow under his head.

In front, a yard or two from the ends of his feet, a small knoll of rock rose out of the grass and moss. It was the barest of knolls, worn and weathered by time and the slow percolations of water. In the centre of it, however, a small pine-tree had sprung up, though how it had succeeded in doing so it was hard to say, since earth, or any receptacle for earth, there was none. From where it sprouted to where his head was pillowed moss grew thickly, and over the moss again was a layer of pine needles, woven together, the ragged ends sticking out here and there like a half-worn door mat. Some small black ants with red tails were slowly struggling over this mat, dragging amongst them the carcase of an earwig many times larger than themselves. John Lawrence fixed his mind upon these ants, and assured himself that he was watching their struggles with the deepest interest. He even went the length of dropping a fragment of grass as a bridge for one of the strugglers. It did not exhibit any particular gratitude, but turned up its red tail in a fighting attitude, and tried to sting first the bit of grass, and then its benefactor's finger. John laughed, threw himself back, and let it take its own way. His next visitor was a bee, which came to visit the flowerets of a vetchling growing in the chinks of the rock. He watched her visiting floweret after floweret in succession, and noticed how she pressed down each till its spring

gave way, and the pollen flew out in a
little cloud as she sent her tongue investi-
gatingly into the purple depths of the
corolla, then, withdrawing it with a dissatisfied hum, flew away to the next and
the next. He looked at all these things,
and assured himself that he was taking the
profoundest interest in them. Another
man, it is true, might not have done so, but
then he had always cared for such things.
Why should he not do so that afternoon?

He had a desperate, a childish idea of
flinging himself upon Nature; of appealing
to her in his trouble; clinging to the
smallest shred of her as a child clings to
its mother's finger; imploring her to keep
off the coming moment; insisting that
she must and should help him, as a pious
Catholic appeals to his patron saint. Had
he not always been loyal to her? might he
not therefore fairly appeal to her in his
need? What good was she, he thought
irascibly, if she could not help him *now?*

It came at last, however—the moment

that he had been fighting off. Nearer and
nearer still, until at last it was impossible
to evade it. It grappled with him, held
him in a grip of iron, and compelled his
attention whether he would or no. Drawn
from his last defences, he rose to his feet
to meet it, as he might have done to meet
a foe.

He loved her! That was all. There was
no possibility of denying or pretending to
deny it any longer. That stage was past
for ever. He loved her utterly; the sound
of her voice, the colour of her eyes, the fall
of her footsteps, her girlishness, immature-
ness, nay, her very follies, her faults. He
loved her, he worshipped her, he believed
that he had always done so; he told himself so, he revelled in the recognition of his
love. Hopeless as it was, ludicrously unavailing as he knew it to be, there was a
joy in repeating it over and over, in escaping—were it but for a moment—out of
himself, out of the realities of things, out
of the cold, revolting present into the

immortal, the ever open Kingdom of Love!

He stretched his arms with a sudden rapture, a sudden sense of deliverance, as if for weeks he had been living cramped between narrow walls from which he had unexpectedly got free; for that moment he was hers, and she was his; his for ever and ever and ever!

It did not last, however; how could it? Like the rush of some wintry torrent, there swept over him a despairing sense of loss, of darkness and ruin. She was lost to him, lost without there having ever been a hope or a possibility of winning her. Lost, and to whom? to that—*that*——

There are moments when the sanest of men cease to be perfectly sane; when the most self-controlled lose hold of themselves; when the wild horses within take the bit between their teeth and will not be gainsaid. This was such a moment to John Lawrence. A rush of bitterness, tenderness, love, jealously, flew through him, not alternately,

but all together, like a pack of wolves. A
flood of hungry longing tore his heart, a
wild desire for happiness, just a little, ever
so little, personal happiness! Why should
he of all the men on earth, he cried to himself, be debarred?

The next instant all these thoughts, too,
were past, swept aside by a flooding tide of
hate—a hate which seemed to spring upon
him like a wild beast, to take him by the
throat, to turn him for the moment into a
wild beast himself. That spasm of jealousy
which had overtaken him in the Palm
garden came again, only with a hundred-
fold force. Again he felt that fierce desire
to snatch her away—if need be by force—
against her own consent—to wrest her away
from him—to assert the old primeval right
of conquest, the right of the better man.
It was a dangerous imagination to let in!
The thought of an encounter with Algernon
Cathers filled his soul with sudden indescri-
bable joy; with a sense of stinging rapture
more intoxicating, perhaps, than even love

itself. His imagination—once allowed to
find entrance—seized upon the idea with
extraordinary vividness, dressed it in its
appropriate colours, and followed it to the
last detail with a breathless absorbing
interest. How, when, where they were to
meet he did not know, what his justification
was to be still less, but he saw the conclusion as clearly as he might have seen it in
a picture, and shuddered even while he did
so. There would come a moment—he knew
there would—when his clutch would be upon
Algernon Cathers' throat, and that hateful
smiling face of his would smile no longer.
He suddenly remembered how once years ago
in India, a tiger-cat had flown at him from
the branch of a tree he was passing under.
There had been no time for anything else,
but he had managed somehow to get his
hand round the beast's throat, and had kept
it there till it was dead, and he recalled
vividly the dull thud of its beautiful supple
body, as he flung it away from him, and it
had dropped in a loose heap upon the ground

—recalled it with a shiver at once of horror and of satisfaction. It would be the very same he said to himself now, the very same !

It was a proof of that underlying savagery, latent under so many disguises, that a man notoriously good-humoured, noticeable even for placidity, should have been thus swept away with passion. Jealousy, and a wild angry sense of impotence, swept backwards and forwards through him, obliterating for the moment all other traits, as the traits of a house are obliterated when a fire gets possession of it. Elly ! Why Elly ? Why must *she* be the one for him to lay his profaning touch upon ? Were there not others, plenty of others, who would have done as well ? Like a flash came back the thought of her as she stood balancing herself a while ago upon the rock ; looking up at him and smiling ; talking of what she had done when she was a child ; so like a child still—so pure, so honest, so clear-eyed. For a moment he half smiled in response, so vivid was the picture, so alive the image his brain had called up. The next minute the smile vanished in a scowl, for beside her, close beside her, leaning over her, absorbing her, holding her hand, pressing his kisses upon her lips, came that other image, the image of the man she was betrothed to, whom she loved—that beautiful smooth-faced smiling young man, Algernon Cathers, with his olive cheeks, and great dark gleaming eyes. He grew sick at the thought, sick and frantic at once. His soul seemed to fill with disgust and loathing, as if he had seen her in contact with something horrible ; something cold, repellent, snaky. Again that spasm of jealousy ran through him, and he shook under it as a man shakes in the first grip of fever. Clasping his hands round a mass of stone, against which he had all this time unconsciously been leaning, he plucked it suddenly from its setting, held it a moment in mid-air, and then flung it away from him with all his force, he knew not why or wherefore. This done he stood watching it with blank

astonishment as it bounded swiftly down
the slope, crushing through a thin covert
of juniper bushes, until it finally subsided
with a thud into some loose earth at the
bottom.

The folly of the act had somehow a sober-
ing effect. He rubbed his hand suddenly
over his eyes. Was *he* behaving like that?
he, John Lawrence, like the hero of some
transpontine melodrama? What had come
to him? Had he gone mad? What sudden
folly had bitten him? It was like looking
in a glass and seeing, not one's own face,
but some one else's, a face with eyes lit up
with demoniac passion. He must go, that
was the next definite idea which occurred to
him. There could be no hesitation about
that *now*. Without a moment's delay he
must get away from this place; from her,
from them all. He had been mad to stay as
long; mad to think that he could go on day
after day seeing her, breathing the same
air—had he not blood in his veins like
another?

For the first time in his life he felt out of his own control. The curb had got twisted somehow, and no longer held. There was no knowing what insanity might not gain possession of him next if he went on exposing himself to this sort of thing; exposing himself to seeing her, to seeing her, too, with him—with that smiling silken puppy who had won her, who would be her master, her husband! Again he stopped, breathing hard and fierce; every drop of blood in his body seemed to be gyrating furiously. Yes, he must get away, he said to himself. There could be no question about it—none. It was too late that day, but the next he would leave Mentone; he had been a fool to remain as long as he had done. If possible he would not see her again. No, upon second thoughts, he would *not* see her again. He would not risk imperilling his honour, her peace of mind, everything still of value by his insanity. He could no longer trust himself. He must go.

Under this fresh impulse he turned to
leave the spot, which seemed to be scored
all over with the traces of his conflict. He
walked down the hill mechanically, with a
trailing step, like that of a man worn out
with prolonged exertion. It seemed as if
hours had passed since he had gone up, yet
the light on the ribs of rock had hardly
shifted an inch, the shadows across the path
were barely if anything longer than they
had been when he mounted.

He had nearly reached the turn of the
path which led to his lodgings, and further
by a back way to the Cather's villa, when
he noticed two figures, those of a man and
a woman, moving a little below him, not
upon the usual pathway, but upon a narrower
track worn by the feet of the olive-pickers.
His glance had travelled indifferently over
them, and was passing away again, when
suddenly it became arrested. Was it?
Nonsense! it could not be, and yet again,
surely, surely it *was* Algernon Cathers—
Algernon Cathers, who had rushed off in

such hot haste two hours ago, to catch the
train for Monte Carlo! The branches of
olive were across the track, so that it was
difficult to see the two figures clearly. Once,
through an opening, he caught a momentary
glimpse of the second one—a tall, handsome-
looking woman, with dark eyes and hair,
apparently a foreigner. The face of her
companion it was impossible to distinguish,
but the general air reminded him of that
fortunate youth. They were sauntering
along, chatting and laughing in very harm-
less fashion; only, if it were Algernon, why
was he there? What the deuce was the
meaning of it all? John Lawrence asked
himself confusedly.

He took out his watch and made a
little mental calculation. Could Algernon
Cathers have gone to Monte Carlo and
returned within the time? It was now
three; it had been one when they parted
upon the esplanade? Yes, it was possible,
just possible; but was it probable? To do
so he must have remained there little more

than half an hour. What likelihood was there of his finding his friend, rescuing him from that despair into which he was said to have been plunged, furnishing him with funds, and returning again within that time? Of course, the friend might have left, something might have occurred to oblige him to return; a hundred things *might* have happened. He was not particularly inclined, however, to give him the benefit of the doubt. If it was Algernon Cathers—and Algernon Cathers, he said to himself, it was, or the devil—then Algernon Cathers had told a lie, one, too, which might be unmasked.

By this time the two figures had disappeared, and with a resolution to put an end to his doubts, the Major rushed after them, crushing through the thick growth of lentisk and rosemary which covered this part of the slope. When he reached the spot where he had seen them last, no one, however, was in sight. He hurried to the next turn, scanning the trees eagerly to

right and left. In the distance he did at
last catch sight of two figures, a man and
a woman; but when, having hurried after
them, he came within speaking distance,
they proved to be only an innocent Mentonese maidservant, and her equally
innocent swain, and he was obliged apologetically to turn back, hot, baffled, and
angry.

He stood still in the middle of the path.
Could his own excited pre-possessions have
had the effect of conjuring up the image of
this man he hated? he wondered. Nonsense,
he told himself; impossible! He had seen
him—he felt certain that he had. Should
he go to Lady Mordaunt and make her the
confidant of his suspicions? He hesitated,
however, to do this. What man alive likes
to be the bearer of such accusations—
especially accusations which might, nay,
probably would be confuted? If Algernon
Cathers had been to Monte Carlo, what
easier than for him to prove that he had
been there, and if so, what sort of a figure

would he himself cut, especially if any hint of the matter came to Elly Mordaunt's ears? Then, indeed, she would be justified in calling him a defamer, a slanderer!

No, he dared not, the risk was too great —the risk of his having after all been mistaken. Were he to speak, and this prove to be the case, how overwhelming would be his own shame, how great the reflected glory of Algernon Cathers! No, bad as the case was, it was not to be cured so. To kill the man out and out and have done with him, he said to himself, was one thing; to bring accusations against him, which might prove to be unfounded, quite another!

He went on to his lodgings, and began to put together his possessions, so as to be in readiness for his departure the next day. Calling the old woman, who, with the aid of her daughter, looked after the house and its inmates, he explained to her that he should not have any need of their services after the following afternoon. About half through his packing he suddenly remem-

bered that it would be necessary also to
give notice to the owner of the house, and
that it would be as well probably to do so at
once. He walked down accordingly to the
town, and left word at the office where he
had hired the rooms, paying a week's rent
in advance of the present time; after which,
being anxious to ascertain the precise time
at which the afternoon train left for Genoa,
he walked on to the railway station.

He had found out what he wanted to
know, and was returning through the
gathering dark, when, at the corner of a
road which a little further back branched
to the hills, he came suddenly face to face,
almost jostling against—Algernon Cathers!
Both men started, even the younger one's
usual imperturbability being momentarily
discomposed—only momentarily, however.

"Bless my soul, Major, how you startled
me! One doesn't expect to see anything
so big in these regions. I suppose you left
Lady Elly at home hours ago?"

"Are you just back from Monte Carlo?"

John Lawrence enquired, answering one question with another.

The young man shrugged his shoulders. "As you perceive," he answered, glancing in the direction of the station. "Had my trip for nothing, too, worse luck! The man had left. I suppose some of M. Blanc's myrmidons paid his fare, as is said to be their amiable custom on these occasions. I have wasted the whole afternoon; I have rubbed shoulders with the nastiest, most disreputable, ugliest, worst-countenanced crew outside the infernal regions. I feel sick, ugly, and disreputable myself; dirty, too, and cross, and not fit to speak to a reasonable being—*ergo*, I will not stay to inflict myself upon you! Bye by! I suppose we shall meet presently at Les Avants?"

He was gone, and John Lawrence, too, walked away after a minute like a man in a remarkably bad dream. Had Algernon Cathers been to Monte Carlo, or had he not? Had he seen him on the hillside, or had he been deceived by some extraordinary vivid resemblance? Thirdly, had the young man just told him a lie—an ugly, uncalled-for, gratuitous lie? Upon the horns of these dilemmas he impelled himself for some time, remaining first on one, and then on the other, as each seemed the least improbable. At last, with a sudden impulse, he flung them all away, as he had flung away the stone upon the hillside. What difference could it make? he said to himself bitterly. Whether Algernon Cathers had or had not told a falsehood upon this particular occasion was really a point of such absolutely infinitesimal importance—a mere thread, straw, feather in the balance. Let him be never so innocent, that would not make him one bit the fitter to be the husband of Eleanor Mordaunt!

He climbed the steps leading to his lodgings still as if in a dream, but once back within its walls he set to work afresh at his packing with a sort of *rabbia*, not resting until everything was stowed away, even to

the strapping of the rugs which lay about the
room. He had a wild desire now to be gone.
The whole place seemed to have suddenly
grown horrible. He felt stifled, gagged,
humiliated, like a man forced by compellent
destiny to sit quietly by and see out the close
of some revolting drama, when every nerve,
and every manly impulse within him is
yearning to cry "stop!"

CHAPTER VII.

WHEN next morning he went to Lady Mordaunt to tell her of his resolution, she received the information at first with less opposition than he expected. She was sitting alone in an armchair upon the terrace, a newspaper in her hands, a screen at one side to cut off the draught, striped awnings over her head, through some narrow slits in which clear-cut pencils of sunlight fell lighting up a spray of loose-petalled roses, lighting up also the rolled-up masses of her hair, looking silvery under the scarf of lace which swept in a loose curve round the back of her neck, leaving the ears and the region of the temples in relief.

" Well, you have been very good," she said, with a half-sigh; " you have stayed here much longer than I dared to hope. I suppose it would not be fair to ask you to sacrifice any more of your time to us."

"It is not that," he said, and then he paused.

"Don't go rushing through Genoa without stopping, as so many people do," she went on in a tone of admonition. "Even with Florence and Rome before you, you ought to give it proper time—a couple of days, at least. There are three or four pictures at the Palazzo Brignole alone which it is part of a liberal education to have seen."

John Lawrence felt an inclination either to laugh or groan, he was not sure which! The idea of his being in the mood to occupy himself with an elaborate scheme of sight-seeing sounded in his ears like a piece of the most grotesque, the most cruelly malicious mockery.

"I don't think somehow I feel particularly keen about picture-seeing," he said grimly.

"Oh, never mind, you will. Like other things, it is only the first step that counts. After the few first Raphaels and Titians you will feel the growing pains of enthusiasm come over you; you will not be able to sleep until you have seen the rest. Shall you get to Venice, do you think?"

"I don't know," he answered gloomily. "No, certainly I shall not go to Venice. Probably it will end by my going straight to Naples, and waiting there till it is time to catch my steamer at Brindisi."

Lady Mordaunt sat bolt upright in her chair, and gazed at him with an air of tragic dismay. "Straight to Naples, without stopping at Florence or Rome! You who have never seen either! Is the man raving? Heaven and earth, you make me blush for my species! Is it conceivable that any one could be so oblivious of what he owes, not to himself merely, but to that civilization of which he is supposed to be a part! I see what it is, though; there is some repulsive sliminess or other, some

creeping crawling abomination, which you
are on thorns to inspect; some octopus, or
revolting sea-slug at that Naples aquarium,
which is more to you than all the pictures
Titian or Michael Angelo between them
ever painted or dreamed of!"

The Major opened his mouth to deny the
accusation, but shut it again without doing
so. In his heart he knew very well that
all the octopuses in creation, nay, all the
accumulated treasures of the zoologic
station, were as little to him then as the
Titians and Raphaels he was supposed to
flout in their favour. There was no knowing, however, what perilous enquiries a
denial might not entail. As well, therefore,
abide under the imputation.

Lady Mordaunt continued looking at him
with the same tragi-comic air of displeasure,
which gradually changed to anxiety as she
scanned him more narrowly. "It strikes
me, do you know, that you are not looking
at all well," she said abruptly. "I wonder
I have not noticed it before. What is the

matter? You are pale. You look like a
man who hasn't slept for a week. Are you
going to have an illness, I wonder? If so,
you had much better stay quietly where
you are and let yourself be nursed like a
Christian?"

"Thank you, I am all right. There is
nothing the matter with me," he answered
hastily.

He was wondering whether to make an
effort to see Elly, or abide by the wiser
resolution of not seeing her again, and con-
tenting himself with a message. Through
the swift rush of this inward colloquy Lady
Mordaunt's voice sounded thin and almost
inarticulate, like a voice upon the other
side of a mountain torrent.

"You are *not* all right, and something *is*
amiss with you. If you are not ill, what is
it?" she answered. "Come, tell me.
Have you had bad news? Have you got
into money difficulties? If so, to so old
a friend—the oldest friend I believe you
possess in the world—you might have the

decency to speak, to give her a chance of
helping you. Come, John, be honest!
Tell me what it is ? ''

"Nothing, I assure you. Indeed, you
are mistaken."

He got up as he spoke and held out his
hand to her. His self-control, he felt,
would not stand many more of these
appeals. If he remained he should be sure
in some way to expose himself, to say
something. Best cut short the interview
while his secret was still his own.

" Will you say good-bye to your—to—to
Lady Eleanor for me ? " he said rather
hoarsely. " I suppose she is out ? "

" Yes, she is out. She has gone out, of
course, with that young man of hers. But
why should I say good-bye to her ? Can't
you say it yourself, to-night ? You do not
propose to desert us because you are
leaving, do you ? Surely you can do your
packing in the morning ! "

" I cannot. You don't understand ; I
have failed to make myself clear. It is

to-day I am going—now—in a few hours—
by this evening's train."

"By this evening's train? You mean
that you have actually come now—*now*, to
say good-bye? No, certainly you did not
make that clear! I don't call that going
away, I call it running away. What have
we done that you should run away from us
in that fashion?"

"You have done nothing, you have only
been too kind—as you always are—but as
I must go, as at the very most I could only
delay a few days longer, I have made up
my mind that it is best to leave at once.
The longer one puts it off the worse it
will be."

"You might have given other people an
opportunity of making up their minds while
you were about it!" she replied indignantly.
"Why did you say nothing of the sort when
you were here yesterday, or the day before,
or the day before that? It was only two
days since you were talking of an expedition
to—I don't know where—some place above

Ventimiglia. Elly has not an idea, I am sure, that you are running away like this. Do you think one parts with a friend as one does with a handful of dead leaves—without five minutes' warning ! "

She gathered her shawl about her shoulders, and moved with an air of resentment towards the doorway. Her resentment was not very long-lived, however. It died upon the threshold. She stopped and turned to look at him, her face softening insensibly, a world of tender regrets filling her blue eyes.

" I wish to Heaven I could keep you for good and all, John," she said gently.

" So do I, with all my heart," he answered. Yet even as he said it he knew that it was not true, that three or four thousand miles of sea and land was the least that it would be safe to put between himself and them ; that anything less would be only tempting him on ; leading him towards that temptation from which he was then fleeing.

" How long, may I ask, do you propose to remain away this time?" Lady Mordaunt went on, with an irritation which did not conceal a very real anxiety to hear the answer.

"I can't say exactly," he answered; " seven years, I suppose, perhaps eight; it depends upon several things. I may be given a staff appointment; I ought, but there is no knowing. Anyhow, I don't see much chance of getting home before seven."

Lady Mordaunt uttered a groan—not a humorous, but a real one, straight from the heart.

" Seven years! How easily he says that! It comes as glibly from his lips as if it were one!" She came back and sat down again in her chair, resting her two arms upon the elbows. " Do you realize, John Lawrence, how very, very unlikely it is that I shall ever set eyes upon you again?" she enquired, looking steadily into his face.

" Don't say that!" he answered; though he knew, of course, that it was true.

She sat a minute in the same attitude, her eyes fixed upon him. Suddenly, to his dismay, her face changed, her lips quivered, and a great tear gathered and rolled slowly over her cheek. He had never seen Lady Mordaunt cry before. He could not even have imagined her doing so; there are women whom one cannot; to whom the shedding of tears seems as improbable an event as to the average man. He had seen her under circumstances which to most women would have seemed to demand a deluge, yet she had never showed a disposition to shed one. It startled him, therefore, even in the midst of his own self-absorbed misery.

"Dear Lady Mordaunt, what is it!" he said, taking her hand. "Pray don't. Have I given you pain? Do tell me what it is. As to my going, of course, that is inevitable, I must go; besides, I cannot flatter myself that is what troubles you. What is it then? Please tell me what this means?"

"It means that I am an old fool, that is what it means," she said, drawing her hand away. "It was not the suggestion of my own decease, by the way, which affected me!" she added, with a gleam of her wonted humour. "Perhaps you may have thought it was, so I may as well inform you that it was not."

"I thought nothing of the kind!" he answered indignantly.

"Neither was it the thought of your departure wholly, though I admit that had something to say to it. It was a mixture of feelings; a sudden sense of—I hardly know what—desolation, perhaps, would be the nearest word; as if a cold wind had blown over me!" She shivered a little and looked about her. "I am rather a lonely old woman, as perhaps you are aware, at least I soon shall be; but what then? all old women are lonely, it is in the nature of things!" She paused; then with a sudden vehemence quite unlike her previous manner, "I wish to God, John

Lawrence, we could break that child's engagement!" she suddenly exclaimed.

"I wish to God we could!" he replied.
Had she guessed how much he *did* wish it?

Lady Mordaunt got up again from her
chair, and took a turn restlessly along the
verandah.

"It is too late—of course, it is too late;
you need not tell me so," she went on
vehemently. "Too late, and I am a fool
to talk, to think even of it." She stopped
and stood facing him, her eyes alight with
fiery grief. "If she would confide in me!
if she would even speak to me of it, I might
do something to convince her of her folly,
or failing that, might try to get reconciled
to it myself! But no, she never alludes to
it! she keeps me at arm's length. I dislike her adorable Prince Perfect; and that
is enough to steel her against me! I am
unworthy even to be spoken to about him.
I am a heretic, an outer barbarian! By
the way, has she ever spoken of him to
you?" she added abruptly.

" Once—yesterday," he replied, rather reluctantly.

" She did ? What did she say ? "

" She said that—that you and I were very unjust to him."

" Unjust ! Heaven grant me patience ! Unjust ! What more ? "

" Not much more. She spoke of his— his good qualities—his amiability, cleverness, generosity. That, I think, was all."

Lady Mordaunt's face was a study. She turned, and began impatiently pacing to and fro.

" I don't believe he cares *that* for her ! " she said, holding out the tip of her finger. " He may think he does, but I don't believe he knows what it means, or could if he tried. He loves himself, that is enough. He marries her because—well, because she is her father's daughter and my granddaughter. Any other Lady Jane, Sukey, Betty would have answered as well. But who is to persuade her of that ? No one ! "

And from the depths of his troubled heart the Major echoed, " No one ! "

Lady Mordaunt stood still; her head a little raised; gleams—fierce, passionate, tender—sweeping by turns over her face.

" Is there *no* way ? " she suddenly exclaimed. " *No* way of getting rid of him ? Couldn't we spirit him off somewhere ? pay somebody to keep him under lock and key ? Not to hurt him, of course, but to keep him out of her sight until her judgment has had time to ripen ? John, help me ! Think ! plot ! plan ! What is the use of your being a *man* if you can do *nothing ?* "

Her eyes were on fire, her hands clenched; she was perfectly serious. For the moment she meant it as genuinely as though she had been some Oriental despot and he her Grand Vizier.

In spite of his own troubles, in spite of that broken heart which he carried in his bosom, in spite of the real misery, trouble, wretchedness of the whole affair, John Lawrence could not forbear a laugh.

"I am afraid that would hardly do!" he said. "We must keep within the law, whatever we do!" Then he approached, and held out his hand to say good-bye. "I mustn't stay; I shall be late; the train leaves in an hour's time. Good-bye, dearest, kindest friend; God bless you. You will say good-bye to—to Lady Eleanor for me?"

His hand was still outstretched, but she for all answer caught his head in both hers and drew it down, kissing brow and cheeks and hair again and again with the passionate clinging kisses of a mother. Then she pushed him suddenly from her, and, turning with a hasty step, ran out of the verandah into the house, disappearing from sight in an instant. And whether she did or did not suspect his secret he never knew.

CHAPTER VIII.

HE got away, and hurried down the now familiar strip of garden, where the mimosas and orange-trees were looking a little pinched with the sudden chill, out of the gate, and along the narrow path which led to the esplanade. At every turn he expected to come face to face with those two whom of all people he least desired then to see. He scanned the approaches in all directions with the eye of a lynx, ready to dash up a flight of stairs, or bolt into a shop, should it be necessary. When he got safely into the less frequented path which led to his own lodgings, he gave a sigh of relief, and yet at the very bottom of his heart disappointment he knew predominated.

He had desired a porter to come for his luggage, which was packed and lying in a heap just inside the entrance. There was nothing to do, therefore, but to wait for his coming, and to smoke a farewell cigar upon the balcony by way of whiling away the interval. The two women were scouring pots and pans upon the little platform which extended a few yards before the kitchen door. He could hear their voices chattering together in that unintelligible gibberish, half French, half Italian, which serves the Mentonese as a medium of communication. Presently the handsome wife of Giacomo came up the lane, and nodded her usual friendly afternoon greeting to him, as he stood there, glum and miserable, looking with haggard eyes over his balcony. That odd sense of permanence in the midst of change which comes over us sometimes when we are in the act of leaving some spot where we have temporally flung grappling irons, was strong upon him. It mingled with those other bitterer,

fiercer preoccupations which were tearing
at his heart. Giannetta's placid nod, her
cheerful certainty of seeing him in the same
place the next day, and the next, and the
next ; the certainty that she, at least, would
come up the same lane day after day, with
the straight black lines of her eyebrows
fronting the sunlight in exactly the same
fashion, and at the self-same hour; the whole
personality of the little scene—the rickety
house in front, with its elaborate network
of cracks, which seemed to have grown
more like the map of some undiscovered
continent ; the cheerful confusion and
slovenliness ; the tall grey peaks overhead,
cold, remote, silent as the thoughts of a
philosopher; the blue arc of sea ; the crowd
of roofs, red, brown, grey—all this tangle
of leafage, of light, and of colour; all this
glittering metallic-looking world—all would
look as it did then, others would see it, *she*
would see it, when he would have wandered
away like a vagrant in his misery. His
sensations just then were those of a vagrant ;

a creature without a home or a tie, without
interest, kindred, friends in the world.
Had he not parted with the last of these.

Too restless to stay where he was, he
flung his cigar away and wandered out into
the lane.   Thoughts beat to and fro without
his being able to direct or control them.
How sweet the girl was! how generous!
What a world of simple, noble impulses—
love and hope and ardent, unhesitating
beliefs—were beating within her, and beating to what an end!   Longings tore him
unceasingly; selfish longings, and longings
that were not altogether selfish.   After all,
he said to himself, what have *you* to complain of?   Toss Cathers aside; fling him by
like some gaudy weed; shut him up for ever,
as Lady Mordaunt proposes, and what then?
How would you be the gainer?   Do you
suppose that she—that young, clear-faced
creature—would spring promptly into *your*
arms? into the arms of a grizzled, undis-
tinguished soldier, a nobody?   And why?
because you knew her when she was twelve

years old! Are you mad? What has become of your sanity, your judgment? Get
you gone to your work. Be thankful that
at least you have work to do. Forget all
this. Leave youth to youth, and be off
with you as quickly as you can!

He was standing now beside a bank rising
steeply out of the lane. A small stream,
led by a tiny wooden aqueduct, was purling
along at the bottom. It had started a
flutter of young green things into sudden
life; arums and narcissus leaves, with
sprays of tall maidenhair standing slim and
erect upon gleaming stalks. John Lawrence
stooped suddenly, and gathered three or
four of these, laying them tenderly away
in a receptacle of his pocket-book, as if they
had been love-tokens. They were, at least,
all the love-tokens he was destined, poor
fellow! to have.

It was a relief that the man who came
to carry his luggage was late, so that there
was nothing to do but to rate him for his
carelessness, help to stow the things on the

barrow, and take a hasty farewell of the old
woman, upon whom he unexpectedly bestowed an extra gratuity, which had the
effect of causing her to follow him to the
edge of the platform with voluble gratitude.

He met nobody he knew on the way to
the station. The very place seemed suddenly to have assumed that air of strange-
ness which often cause the first and last
impression of a place to wear a family resemblance. His railway carriage was
crammed to suffocation with Germans, two
solid, silent men, and three equally solid,
but, unfortunately, not equally silent women,
who gabbled guttural notes of admiration
within a few inches of his ears. It was
impossible to secure a window, and though
he stood up at the moment of starting, and
leaned forward, " Les Avants" refused to
disentangle itself from the cluster of houses.
To make amends the " Villa Splendide"
stood out in full relief, that knoll upon
which he had stood with Mrs. Cathers, and

seen her son and Elly Mordaunt emerge out
of the shrubbery below, being the last piece
of Mentone which presented itself to his
eyes.

In spite of Lady Mordaunt's injunctions
he did not remain at Genoa. It was too
near; he could not. He had a feverish
desire to get away as far as possible; as it
were to the very ends of the earth. He
spent two days at Florence and two more
at Rome, and he walked across the Ponte
Vecchio at the former, and strayed into the
Coliseum at the latter. This is all the
sight-seeing that can be set down to his
credit, anything else being purely involuntary, merely such flotsam and jetsam as the
chances of the road floated before his eyes.

At Naples, however, not a little to his own
dismay, he fell into the hands of a cicerone,
who insisted upon doing for him what he
had neither the capacity nor the will to do
for himself. This was a certain Signor
Golfino, one of the staff of naturalists who
have made it their headquarters, and with

whom about a year before he had had a slight correspondence upon some point of marine zoology. The Major had forgotten the very name of his enthusiastic correspondent whose confident English at the time had been a source of some little amusement to him. Although he had forgotten Signor Golfino, Signor Golfino had apparently not forgotten him, and no sooner did his name appear in the visitors' list of his hotel than that amiable enthusiast hastened to call upon him, insisting with all the kindliness of his nation and the friendliness of a brother scientist, upon doing the honours of Naples in general, and the zoologic station in particular, to the new-comer.

It bored him frightfully at the time, but there is no doubt that it did him good. Escaped from this amiable tyranny, his thoughts reverted with the precision of a released spring to that image which filled them exclusively. Every saying of hers, however unimportant, every word or deed,

however little worth recalling, being passed
over and over in review, made to give up
the very utmost meaning which by any
ingenuity could be extracted from them.
How little it was after all! With that self-
pity which comes to a man inevitably under
such circumstances, he could not help
reflecting upon the extraordinary fatality
which out of the whole world of womankind
had caused him to set his heart so tenaciously upon just this one. It did seem the
most gratuitous piece of misery to have
inflicted upon himself! That Elly—the
little girl whose image had been such a
pleasantly placid possession, a soothing
green spot in the somewhat arid field of
his memory—that *she* should have become
a source of such bitter, such unavailing
misery—a misery which haunted his days
with its remorseless pang, and woke him up
twenty times at night to impale him afresh
upon its thorns.

He found a letter from her at Naples,
written to wish him good-bye, since, as she

said, he had not given her an opportunity
of doing so in person, which she did not
think was *kind*. It was a very simple little
effusion, almost as much so as those he
had been in the habit of getting some four
or five years earlier, in which the rabbits
and ponies and wood-pigeons filled the
greater part of the loosely scrawled pages.
It gave him a good deal of pleasure, though,
as will be conceived, a good many heart-
stings, too. The more he thought of her
future the more he felt that she was floating
blindly, unhesitatingly, joyously into—well,
into what? He hardly, even now, knew,
but something certainly very different from
what she so radiantly anticipated. Apart
from his own troubles his heart bled for
her. The lip of the cataract was so green,
and smooth, and pleasant, but once she had
crossed it !—— Well, thank God, he said
to himself, he should not be there to see !

Released from the irritation of his presence, he tried to reason down the inveterate
dislike and suspicion with which that too

successful young man, Algernon Cathers,
had inspired him. It cannot be said that
his efforts were remarkably successful. That
the dislike was chiefly what is called in-
stinctive he was obliged to own. It was
not founded on reason, for even if certain
traits seemed to support it, they were hardly
of sufficient blackness to bear exposure to
the daylight without, in some degree, losing
their damnatory character. It was an antipathy of nerves and heart, rather than
of head, but as such only the less to be
argued away or diminished. Seeing, however, that nothing that he could say or do
would avail to save her; that none of those
whose business it was to shield her ignorance and protect her innocence, seemed
able or willing to do so; that, on the contrary, most of them were urging her forward
with acclamations of eager approval. Seeing
all this, the only possible, the only manly
thing he told himself to do, was to hope
that the scales might never fall from her
eyes; that love, imagination, *something,*

might so gloss over those pitfalls which
yawned before her, that she might practically never perceive them; never know
how unlike this man she had bound herself
to marry was to that imaginary being, born
of fancy and a young girl's impressionable
generosity, whom she had taught herself
to love. It was after this fashion that he
tried to face the catastrophe which had
shaken his life out of all its settled ways,
and flung it, a maimed and broken thing,
upon his hands, and it was in this mood,
or as near an approach to it as he could
achieve, that he finally set sail upon New
Year's Day for his little loved duties in
India.

BOOK IV.

BACK AGAIN.

CHAPTER I.

OVER the proceedings of the next six years John Lawrence's chronicler may be allowed to pass with a hasty step. Within a few months of his return to India he received that staff appointment of which he had spoken to Lady Mordaunt—one of those posts beginning with the words " Deputy Adjutant," which to non-military ears all sound precisely alike. It was a good appointment, and a well-paid one, as Indian appointments for the most part are, and he remained in it for some three years, and would have remained another two but for a call to return to his regiment, in order to grapple with one of the worst onslaughts of cholera which had visited that part of

India for nearly a quarter of a century. The Colonel was away on leave, the next man in command fell ill, and John Lawrence hastily decided to resign his own appointment and return with all speed to his post in the regiment.

That he did not himself succumb to the malady it is needless to say, but when the worst was over, and the foul fiend had withdrawn, glutted, if not satiated with its tale of victims, his strength was at a point of prostration which in all his previous vigorous manhood he had never even imagined approaching. He had a touch, too, of jungle fever, and the two together brought him very low, so low, that the doctor insisted on complete cessation from all work as his only chance of thorough recovery. He fought against this decision as long as he could. Deep as was his dislike of India—a dislike which seemed to increase with every year—there were many reasons that made him anxious to remain where he was for the present, and to resume his staff appointment. There came a moment, however, when the doctors became peremptory. It was go, or die, they said, and on the whole it seemed better, therefore, to go. Colonel Lawrence—he had become a brevet-Colonel, by the way, two years before—received a twelvemonth's leave, with an understanding that more would be forthcoming should it be needed, and about the middle of March set sail in a P. and O. steamer from Bombay.

His first intention had been to take passage in a troop-ship, but this virtuous resolution he at the last moment threw over, and elected to return by the costlier and more expeditious route. He had a wish—into the motives of which he did not take the trouble to dive too deeply—to return to England as he had left it, namely *via* Italy, and in this he had been encouraged by the doctor, who warned him against confronting the proverbial treachery of an English April.

It was the mere ghost of John Lawrence

that came on board, but the voyage and
his own good constitution between them
performed wonders, so that by the time he
disembarked at Venice he began to look
upon himself in the light of an impostor,
and to ask himself whether, if this state of
affairs proved permanent, honesty would not
require him to cancel his own leave, and
return to his duties with as little delay as
possible.

The six years which had passed since his
return had produced changes in his position
in more ways than one. If he still did not
love his banishment, at least he endured it
better. For one thing, he had grown to
find that interest in his profession which a
fairly intelligent man can hardly fail to find
in any work, however little originally sympathetic, into which his best capabilities are
perforce driven. For the first time, too,
those capabilities had found recognition.
He stood high in the regard of those with
whom he had worked, and in whose hands
advancement lay. His career in India was

a widely different thing from what it had
been when he had last breathed Italian air.
If his health lasted he had only to return,
and, within the limits of that branch of the
service to which he stood committed, there
were few posts that might not, sooner or
later, be open to him.

On the other hand his home ties had
suffered the fate of all ties which are divided,
not more by distance than by an utter
severance of all interests and pursuits. His
younger brothers he had not heard of for
more than a year. They were well, he believed, and prosperous he hoped, but beyond
that he knew little or nothing about them.
His step-mother, and her two little girls,
were settled at Brighton, to their own ap-
parent satisfaction. His brother William,
with whom he at stated periods inter-
changed letters, had migrated to another
parish not far from a cathedral town. Lady
Mordaunt, the only person with whom he
kept up a steady correspondence, was
settled, he knew, in her old home in Devon-

shire, and, in spite of those prognostica-
tions which had heralded his departure, was
well, and likely to welcome him with as
vigorous a kindliness as she had done eleven
years earlier.

Through her he had been kept fairly *au
courant* as to the proceedings of the other
members of her family, though there was a
tone of reserve about her letters of which
he had not in earlier days been conscious.
Her grand-daughter's marriage had taken
place some six months after he had sailed,
and she had, therefore, now been married a
little over five years.

There were two children, a girl and a boy,
about whom their great-grandmother wrote
in terms of modified grandmotherly rapture.
Algernon Cathers' health was occasionally
alluded to, and he gathered that it was a
source of some anxiety to his wife, though
nothing was said that led him to suppose
that there was any actual call for alarm;
indeed, John Lawrence had heard so much
in his time about Algernon Cathers' ill-

health, that the conclusion he had rather
uncharitably come to was that a full half of
it was imaginary, and that he was destined
to outlive most of his less-talked-of contem-
poraries.

Lady Mordaunt's habitual frankness had
not gone the length of lifting the veil which
shrouded her grand-daughter's married life,
so that he had been left to gather such
intimations as he could by that irritating
process known as reading between the lines,
one which results, we all know, in alternative
and often diametrically opposite impressions,
according to the frame in which we happen
to approach it. Throughout his journey,
the idea of returning to England *via* Genoa
and Marseilles, and in that case of halting
at Mentone, where the Cathers were still,
he knew, encamped in their winter quarters,
had presented itself with much iteration to
his thoughts. He could not, however, re-
solve upon doing so. He wished, yet shrank
from it. The idea of knocking at that
particular door; being shown in; finding

them together; going through the forms
of cordiality; seeing himself — however
temporarily — a guest under Algernon
Cathers' roof! No, he said to himself,
no ! There were some things a man could
not do, which no man ought to *ask* himself
to do.

Athough the first tide of love, and wrath,
and impotent hatred had long since ebbed
away and given place to healthier and more
reasonable sentiments, there was enough
soreness still to make him shrink from
exposing himself to such an ordeal. To see
them together would be productive of one
of two things. Either he would grow
reconciled, which could hardly fail to entail
some loss of ideal, or he would not be at
all reconciled, and the old wounds would
begin to bleed afresh, the old bitterness be
accentuated tenfold. If he were to see her
unhappy, perhaps even unkindly treated by
that—*that*—. Years, it will be observed,
had not diminished the vigour of our hero's
prejudices, and that significant blank,—

more expressive, perhaps, than most oppro-
brious epithets—was still what in his own
thoughts he oftenest applied to Eleanor
Cathers' husband. A man may be robbed
of what to him represents all womankind,
yet, after the first rush of rivalry, cease to
detest his rival. In John Lawrence's case
the elements were less simple. He would
have disliked Algernon Cathers, probably,
in any case, but his dislike had been in-
creased and multiplied tenfold by suspicion.
He suspected him of he knew not what, and
even now, when years appeared to have
disproved his suspicious, he suspected him
still. If with an effort he could have got
over this dislike he would, perhaps, have done
so, but he knew himself better than to suppose it possible, and therefore made no such
futile attempt. It was with these alternate
impulses plucking with little diminished
energy at his heart that he arrived one
gusty April night at Genoa, leaving the
further direction of his journey still un-
determined.

His train was late, and the transit to the
hotel was accomplished in a huge rattling
omnibus which smelt of boots, and none of
the windows of which could be induced to
open. He was the only passenger, the big
unwieldy thing rocking its way between
walls which rose like beetling crags upon
either side of the narrow street. The hotel
too, when attained, proved to be of size
proportionate to the vehicle belonging to
it. And when, having swallowed a hasty
meal, he was conducted to a gusty cavern
of a bed-room, and left there to the light of
a single candle, half extinguished by the
gusts which swept through door and window,
he retired to bed in a frame of mind dis-
tinctly the reverse of amiable.

Next morning brought relief. His sepul-
chral bedroom proved to be provided with
a balcony, upon which, on the strength of
his invalidship, he allowed himself to break-
fast. The sun shone ; the air was warm,
yet tingling ; below him the sweep of the
harbour extended itself in all its magnificent

amplitude, the new pier stretching out a friendly arm to meet its older and less imposing brother. Our Colonel felt a sudden desire to inspect all this at closer quarters, so sallied out prepared for enjoyment, and determined to find it.

As his biographer has before remarked, he was not artistically gifted, and things had need to be very picturesque in order to impress themselves upon his mind as such. Genoa, however, upon this occasion performed the feat—perhaps because he was in the mood to allow it to do so. He told himself that he liked it better than Venice, a sentiment which, I fear, only displays the depth of his æsthetic depravity. The fact was that his long continued spell of weakness and depression had suddenly taken an upward turn, and Genoa reaped the credit. Convalescence is a period either of great depression or of great exuberance, and having long been the former, it had now become the turn of the latter. He felt well, or upon the high road to be well; he felt, too,

that blissful premonition of happiness which
comes to us sometimes by the merciful
favour of heaven without a grain of anything
in our circumstances to call it forth. He
revelled in the sense of being once again on
European soil, and he looked towards the
line of Rivieran headlands melting one
behind the other, with a tenderness which
for the moment carried no bitterness with it.

Tired at last of the clatter and jostle, he
lounged up the broad steps of the Terasso
di Marmo, and sat down on a stone bench
in one of the small recesses that break the
long line of its marble balustrade. It was
very still and hot, too hot for any one not
already seasoned to a yet fiercer radiance.
The broad white expanse wore an odd resemblance to a sheet of ice, starred by small
cracks, and glittering under a sunshine
which awakened queer distorted reflections
like sudden impish smiles at the corners.
Upon the whole expanse not a creature was
to be seen except a slovenly girl with a red-
and-green plaid shawl over her black head,

who was sauntering along with a listless
slip-shod step, munching cherries as she
went, and throwing their stalks away over
the marble parapet. Between the pillars
of the balustrade he could see into the
arcades below, in one of which some men
were beating and twisting bars of red-hot
iron, the red glow of the forge behind
giving them no little resemblance to some
of those painstaking demons we see in certain of the great damnatory canvases. The
Colonel did not think of this, but it struck
him they must be deuced hot down there.

When he looked back the Terraso was no
longer deserted. The woman with the plaid
shawl had departed, but four other figures
had taken her place, and were advancing
slowly towards him over its smooth expanse.
These consisted of a tall lady, carrying a
large white sunshade and leading a little girl
by the hand ; a stout personage, evidently
a nurse, who, when John Lawrence first
perceived the party, carried a child in her
arms, which being set down up m its feet,

had begun to toddle with fat uncertain legs
over the pavement, its diminutive shadow
waving an uncertain and wobbling ac-
companiment upon the gleaming surface.

The lady with the sunshade advanced
directly towards him; the little girl—a tiny
elfin-like creature, with a mass of fair hair
set on end like an electrical doll's—running
beside her. Both were looking over the
harbour as if amongst that inextricable mass
of boats, sails, and spars, seeking to distinguish some one sail or spar in particular.
When nearly on a line with him, the lady
glanced carelessly towards him, and was in
the act of passing on, but seemed suddenly
arrested as if struck by some singularly vivid
resemblance, the next minute averting her
gaze as if aware of having made a mistake.
She had not gone half-a-dozen steps, however,
before she again paused, and looked back
with an air of uncertainty. The Colonel
on his side had risen and was looking after
her with a vague stupefaction, a growing
bewilderment, through which faint thrills

of memory were beginning to throb and burn. This time she no longer hesitated. She turned round, letting the child's hand go as she did so, and advanced towards him, with the liberated hand extended.

" Surely you will not tell me that I am mistaken! Surely you *are* Major Lawrence?" she said.

" Lady Eleanor!" It all rushed over him like a flood, without warning, without a single moment's breathing time. Now that she had spoken, recognition followed as a clap follows a flash. Even now, however, he could hardly blame his own amazing stupidity, so greatly had she altered. She was always tall, but even her height seemed to have changed its character, the six years that had intervened having quite robbed it of that youthful angularity which had made it a defect rather than an embellishment. Her face, too, had greatly changed, and changed, there was no question, immeasurably for the better. There had been far less difference between the child of

twelve and the girl of seventeen, than there
was between the girl of seventeen and the
woman of twenty-three. She was a beautiful woman now, strikingly, unquestionably
beautiful, far more so than she had promised
to be. And yet—so strangely are men made
—the first effect of this realization was a
sudden sense of intense disappointment,
followed almost instantly by one of relief.
He had dreaded this meeting, dreaded it
more than he had avowed to himself, but now
he suddenly perceived that he dreaded it
no longer. Elly Mordaunt,—the child, the
girl whom he had loved and lost—was gone,
vanished ! It was as though she had never
existed. This beautiful, stately, benign-
looking young woman who stood before him
was not his Elly at all. She was Lady
Eleanor Cathers, quite a different person,
another man's wife, and the mother of these
children ; no more perilous to his peace of
mind, he told himself, than yonder mosaic
Madonna up on that palace wall, and in the
exhilaration produced by this sudden realiza-

tion he was able to respond to her greeting
with a warmth and appropriateness which
he would otherwise have found impossible.

She, however, was the first to speak.

"This is wonderful!" she exclaimed.
"I cannot help feeling that I am speaking
to a ghost! When did you leave India?
It was only the other day that my grandmother wrote to say that she had heard
from you, and that you had been ill, but not
a word about your coming home!"

"No, it was a sudden thought. I seemed
to be getting worse, so was packed off
without being allowed an opinion on the
subject. Now I find that, as I suspected,
it was all a mistake, and that I am here
under false pretences. In fact, I think I am
bound in honour to return!"

"I wouldn't do that. I don't think you
look at all too well!"

"Well, I am not starting immediately, at
any rate! And you, Lady Eleanor? I can
hardly believe in my own good fortune!
That within two days of my landing in

Europe, I should meet you face to face! If it is strange to you to see me, think what it is to me to see you!"

"Oh, but my being here is not really so strange," she answered in her old, serious, eager tones. "We are often in Genoa. It is not far, you know, from Mentone, and my husband likes moving about. He gets tired, naturally, of the long dull winter always in the same place. I have left him now at the hotel, and came with the children to look for the yacht; it was to have come in last night from Mentone. Jan, darling, come here and speak to this gentleman. Do you know this is a very, very old friend of mother's, who knew her when she was very little older and not much wiser than you are?"

Jan, whose big eyes looked up with an air of preoccupation from under her cloud of hair, was a wee child with a small old-fashioned face, too pale to be pretty, but with an air of preternatural wisdom which belied her mother's words.

"How do you do?" she said in a small, distinct voice, with the due emphasis upon every separate syllable. "Please, where ith the *Veda?*" pointing a small finger anxiously towards the harbour.

"Jan's one thought day and night is the *Veda*," her mother said, smiling. "I say we keep it for her benefit, as my husband is so seldom able to go sailing. No, Jan dear, this gentleman does not know where the *Veda* is, and we must wait till we get back to find out where she was to anchor."

"How old is she?" the Colonel enquired with a smile.

"A little past four. She is a mite, is she not, even for that age?"

"She looks very big to me when I remember that she is your daughter," he answered.

"Ah, yes! It makes one feel very old, doesn't it?" she said lightly, after which there was a moment's pause.

"You will come back with us to the hotel?" she added entreatingly. "You cannot imagine what a happiness it is seeing you again! Do you know I was feeling this morning as if something pleasant was going to happen? One doesn't often have that feeling, once one has left off being a child, does one? but to-day, oddly enough, I had."

"I had just the same," he answered, smiling.

They went down the broad steps, little Jan still turning wistful eyes towards the sea, and pulling at her mother's hand to make her go slower. An open carriage was waiting at the foot of the steps, into which they all got; the children first, then the nurse, then Lady Eleanor and the Colonel. It seemed to him the strangest piece of unreality to see her settling them upon the seat opposite, ascertaining with all a mother's solicitude that the wraps were properly tucked round little knees, and the parasols tilted at exactly the right angle to hinder the sun from striking upon small eyes blinking up at the daylight. Was it,

could it be Elly Mordaunt? his own wild,
untamed, untamable Elly? he asked himself; she who only yesterday was a child
herself? or was he indulging in the
strangest, the most extravagant of day-
dreams? Surely, surely the latter!

CHAPTER II.

THE hotel to which they were driven was
at some distance from his own, and was
situated in one of the larger squares. The
Cathers' rooms — a much-decorated suite,
with enormously heavy gilt furniture—were
upon the first floor, and were approached
by a staircase hung with pictures, more
gorgeous, perhaps, than valuable. Young
Mr. Cathers was lying upon a sofa near
the open window, but sprang up immediately
upon their entrance, and shook hands
cordially with his wife's companion. He
had not changed much, the Colonel thought;
his complexion was more waxen, and he was
thinner than he had been, otherwise there
was not much difference. He was nearly

as handsome, and as soon appeared not a whit less conversational than of old.

There was a great clatter of buying and selling going on under the windows, the greater part of the piazza being littered with cabbage-stalks and odds and ends of greenery, with men and women, too, engaged in pulling down and packing up numerous booths and movable counters. It seemed to offer a natural topic of conversation, and John Lawrence made some remark about it. Algernon Cathers at once took up the lead:

"Insufferable, is it not?" he exclaimed, seating himself again upon his sofa with an air of dramatic despair. "Italy is the noisiest country in the world, and Genoa the noisiest town in Italy, and this hotel the noisiest in all Genoa! We have changed our rooms three times since we arrived here, but always for the worse. When we first came our bedrooms looked to this side, and the roaring and rattling continued till long past midnight, and

began again with the first ray of daylight.
Then—thinking that nothing could be
worse—I made them move us to the back,
but if I did I found that a *vicolo*, as I
believe they call the thing, runs exactly
there, and up and down it the people pour,
stopping now and then to cluster under the
window in knots to discuss the welfare of
Italy, added to which the infernal thing
is paved with stones or bricks, which stick
out in ribs all the way down, so that every
truck and barrow that passes seems to be
going jog, jog, jog, over your unfortunate
vertebral column. Then, thinking that we
must at last have attained the uttermost
depths of pandemonium, I made them
change us once again, but, will you believe it, I find that there are huge iron
cages full of cocks and hens fastened on to
the outside of the house opposite — about
two feet away — and the cackling and
crowing of those miserable fowls is enough
to cause the very dead to rise up out of
their graves to swear. I wanted to practise

at them with a saloon pistol, but Lady
Eleanor wouldn't hear of it, and the hotel
manager wrings his hands and declares that
he can do nothing, as they don't belong to
him, so there is nothing to do but put up
with it as long as we stay, and oscillate
from one room to the next, according as the
noise becomes more endurable upon one
side or the other. At present it seems to
be worst here, so I vote we move to the
other sitting-room."

"It will be better soon; the market
seems nearly over, Algernon," said his wife.

"Better! But for how long? You people
without nerves don't know your own good
fortune! I believe you'd as soon have the
cocks and hens as not! Meanwhile it must
be luncheon time. You'll stay luncheon,
Major, of course?"

But the Colonel hastily excused himself,
declaring that he never ate luncheon.

"Not even if you call it tiffin? I
thought all Indians ate tiffin. Anyhow,
don't go, or we shall lose sight of you for

ever. What were you going to do this afternoon? Can't we combine and go somewhere together? For Heaven's sake, don't desert us! Remember that we are stranded mariners, and that you are a friendly sail that has just hoved in sight!"

"I was thinking of going to the Campo Santo. That seems to be one of the sights," John answered.

"The Campo Santo! That's a lively place for a man to go to! The doctors tell me I shall take up my residence there soon for good and all, if I don't mind, so I think I'd better keep out of it as long as I can."

"Oh, yes, don't let us go to the Campo Santo!" Lady Eleanor said hastily.

"After all, though, I don't see why not," her husband rejoined. "It's one of the regular Genoese sights, as Lawrence says, and having been here some twenty times, it's rather a disgrace never to have seen it. Who's afraid? I'm not. If you and the Major—— Not Major? What then? Oh, of course, Colonel, thousand apologies! If

you and the Colonel will take your chances,
I am game to do so. You can take that
portentously serious little daughter of yours
too, if you like. Such a piece of solemnity
will be quite in her place amongst the
tombstones ! "

The Colonel looked apologetically at Lady
Eleanor. He was sorry he had mentioned
the place, as it was evident that she had
a dislike to going there. She made no
further objection however.

"What o'clock shall we order the
carriage ? " she inquired of her husband.

"Any hour Lawrence likes. He is the
visitor, the passer-by. Happy man, I wish
I was ! We are the logs, sticking in a
backwater while all the rest go floating by."

The carriage was standing before the
door of the hotel when, an hour later, John
Lawrence returned, and they were speedily
driving between the unattractive-looking
houses which congregate about the Porto
Romano, and through that aperture into
the sudden view of fort-crowned hills which

surround the town. The horses were
so good, the carriage rattled over the indifferently paved road at such a remarkable
pace, that he could not forbear remarking
upon it. The mystery became less surprising, however, when it was explained
that carriage and horses were the Cathers'
own; they had brought them with them
from Mentone. "It saves a world of
bother," their owner explained.

Getting down at the entrance to the
cemetery their passage was impeded for a
moment by a stout gentleman with a broad
red neck and large white necktie, who,
upon turning round, was greeted by the
Cathers as Mr. Nokes. From the conversation that ensued it appeared that this
gentleman was also a winter inhabitant of
Mentone, where he had left his family and
come away for a few days' relaxation;
indeed, the Colonel, to whom he was
introduced, thought that he vaguely re-
collected his face as that of one of the
habitués of Lady Mordaunt's salon.

Lady Eleanor, who seemed anxious to keep by her husband's side, led the way with him into the open part of the cemetery, the other two gentlemen following, little Jan running on ahead, and pausing every now and then, like a small pointer, to stare solemnly at some object which caught her attention, looking back as she did so at her mother to make her examine it too.

Your first visit to these parts, Colonel Lawrence ? " Mr. Nokes inquired hospitably. There was something genial about his rubicund, singularly ugly face, close-shaven like a Roman priest's, but in which the fatherly element seemed to predominate over the sacerdotal.

The Colonel explained that he had passed through Genoa before, but that circumstances had then obliged him to hurry, so that he knew little or nothing of its attractions.

"Ah—interesting town, very ! Now this place "—glancing comprehensively at the

long grey corridors and central space be-
dotted with tombstones—"this place, I
suppose, has certainly no equal in the
world. The mere amount of money which
people expend upon these mementoes is
something phenomenal—particularly if you
take their poverty into consideration.
Regrettable you say? Well yes, regrettable,
if you look at it in one way, but still
interesting, decidedly interesting. It
makes them reflect too, no doubt, and
must have a good effect in that respect.
By the way, I was a little surprised, do you
know, to meet Mr. Cathers here," he added,
dropping his voice to a significant whisper,
and glancing at his companion as he did so.

Colonel Lawrence looked at him inquiringly.

"Mr. Cathers? Yes. I was surprised,
I say, to see him here. He has always
seemed to me to shrink from anything that
recalled—anything suggestive of death, you
know; to be decidedly morbid and nervous
upon the subject. Sad, but not, perhaps, so

very unnatural. Not having any regular
spiritual duty at Mentone, I have hesitated
to touch upon the subject with him, in
fact, should hardly have felt myself justified
in doing so, but that has always been my
impression. You are aware, I suppose, that
the doctors have a very bad opinion of him,
are you not?" he added abruptly, sinking
his voice to a complete whisper, and
glancing cautiously ahead, so as to make
sure that the other three were out of ear-
shot.

"I was not, indeed. I know that his
chest has always been delicate, and that he
is obliged to winter abroad, but not that
there was anything seriously amiss."

Mr. Nokes shook his head slowly from
side to side, compressing his large loose lips
as he did so.

"It is so, I assure you. His lungs are
——" he tapped his own broad chest, and
shook his head again with an air of concern.
"If he is alive this time next year it will
be a miracle; nothing short of a miracle,"

he said impressively. "Dr. Mulligan all but admitted as much to me."

"Good God! you don't say so?" John Lawrence exclaimed.

He looked up suddenly at the husband and wife walking side by side some twenty yards ahead of them. Algernon Cathers was laughing and pointing to something with his stick, she smiling in response. It was not in itself an enlivening scene. Hundreds of more or less grim little symbols of death were sprouting like mushrooms out of the grass, every little column or squat cross bearing its burden of dusty immortelles, or more deplorable withered flowers, each with a black lantern dangling like a felon's effigy from a peg in the ground beside it. Not a cheerful scene as to its details, and yet, taken as a whole, flooded as it was with sunshine, with here and there a bright patch of colour; with the violet hills behind crowned with forts; with the sea catching the eye through a sudden dip in the ground, it looked bright

and smiling enough ; a piteous commentary
in its brightness upon this sentence which
he had just heard pronounced. Like most
self-contained men, John Lawrence had
great capabilities of hatred, and he had
hated this young man as he had certainly
never hated any one else in his whole life.
For all that, as he looked at him now, a
great wave of pity seemed to rise and sweep
over him ; to engulph and almost to extin-
guish his hatred. In a year ! To leave
wife, children, fortune—everything that
could make life happy—and to go out into
the cold ; into the void ; naked ; alone !
A man so luxurious ; so spoilt ; who had
never in all his life had to do anything he
disliked. The horror of the thing struck
home to him vividly, and he shuddered
with a sudden rush of pity.

" Does his—do you suppose Lady Eleanor
knows ? " he enquired hoarsely.

" I fancy so. At least I have always
seemed to read the secret of her extraordinary patience in some such knowledge,"
Mr. Nokes replied.

The Colonel's pity, which was flowing in a warm flood, seemed suddenly to congeal as if smitten with frost. "You mean that he —doesn't—doesn't treat her well?" he enquired, dropping his voice to an even lower key than they had hitherto spoken in. "Excuse the question," he added abruptly. "I dare say it seems to you that I have no right to put it, but I am a very old friend, and I only returned two days ago from India, so you may imagine I am naturally anxious to know anything that affects her —their interests."

Mr. Nokes' cheerful rubicund face assumed an air of responsibility. "I really— I am no authority," he said, rather shortly. "As I said, my acquaintanceship has been a matter purely of externals. I have no pretension to call myself a friend. What I know is obvious to every one. He is an invalid who will not be treated like an invalid, and yet that abuses the privileges of invalidship. To keep him in humour must be a very serious task. Lady Eleanor is entitled to every one's sympathy."

The Colonel longed to ask more. It seemed an opportunity which might not recur of getting to know the facts about Algernon Cathers as they were known to the outer world. Yet what right or authority, after all, had he to ask ? He was still inwardly debating the matter when they were summoned by a call from the party in front, who had stopped before a monument placed near the entrance of one of the galleries. This monument represented a stout Genoese citizen ascending up to heaven, arrayed in his dress-clothes, complete down to the boot-buttons, and supported on either side by a pair of dumpy cherubs, their cheeks ornamented with tears of the dimensions of hazel-nuts. The defunct gentleman was being waited for on high by an expectant galaxy of saints, while below his despairing family stood about in attitudes expressive of distinguished woe, their tasselled boots and other adornments conscientiously rendered. The adoring wife, while straining her eyes after her ascending lord, being careful to

lift her upper skirts an inch or two, so that
the sculptor might not fail to impress upon
the spectators his perfect ability to grapple
with the difficulties presented by a third
and even a fourth layer of embroidery which
ornamented the flounces of her petticoat.

"There you behold the quintessence of
modern Italian art!" Algernon Cathers was
saying as they came up. "Look at their
hooks-and-eyes! look at their eyelet-holes
and tassels and bobbins! look at their
brooches and gloves, and eyelashes and
hairpins! Can't you imagine with what
pride the survivors must come here upon a
Sunday afternoon, and count the buttons
upon their own boots, and point out to
their friends exactly the attitudes they took
upon the interesting occasion! Eleanor,
my dear, this is *not*, by the way, the style
of monument which I wish you to erect in
my honour," he continued, turning with
mock solemnity to his wife. "Mr. Nokes,
I take you to witness!"

In the light of the information he had

just received, that piece of pleasantry
sounded ghastly in John Lawrence's ears,
more ghastly if anything than the sepul-
chral ornamentations of the place, and he
moved a step aside to examine a bust which
stood upon a pedestal hard by.

Algernon Cathers, too, seemed to have
had about enough of the Campo Santo.
His glance, which had been smilingly roving
from group to group, was suddenly arrested
by a skull grinning with hollow cavernous
jaws above a pair of cross-bones, and he
gave a quick involuntary shiver. "Come,
it is late," he said abruptly; "Miss Jan
ought to be getting home to her tea. Ugh!
what an ugly place it is, to be sure! Thank
Heaven, we've done it once and for all!"

He lingered again, however, a little further on, fascinated as most visitors are by
the grisly humours of the scene. Lady
Eleanor walked ahead, holding her little
girl by the hand, and John Lawrence
availed himself of the opportunity to say a
few words to her apart.

"I am afraid you don't thank me for having suggested this expedition," he said apologetically.

"Oh, don't think that. It is one of the regular sights, and we should have had to come sooner or later. Only all this panoply of woe, this deliberate elaboration of broken-heartedness seems to me to make death and sorrow so much uglier and more painful. It is as if the people were grimacing and posturing for one's admiration—like those skeletons decked in fine clothes one sees in some of the frescoes! Still, as we should have had to come and see it some day, it is as well, as Algernon says, to get it over. You are not leaving Genoa just yet, I hope?" she added, with rather a hasty change of subject.

"I am not sure," he answered doubtfully. "Do you expect to remain much longer?"

"A week, perhaps more, I cannot tell. We are forbidden to return to England before the end of May, and it is very difficult to fill the time up satisfactorily. Alger-

non likes staying within reach of the yacht,
though we are able to make so little use of
it. We lunch on board occasionally, or
take little cruises when it is very calm."

" You used not to mind rough weather."

" No, but Algernon is forbidden to go out
when there is any wind, there is always a
danger of it irritating his lungs. Probably
when we leave here we shall go to Spezia.
One can sail about the bay there almost
any day, and it is warmer than here. This
Genoa climate is the most treacherous
thing possible. Just now it is warm enough,
but any moment the wind may become
piercing."

" Spezia is rather a nice place, is it
not ? " the Colonel said tentatively.

" Yes, at least it used to be. You don't
know it ? Come and make acquaintance
with it. Unless, that is, you have any
urgent business to do in England. Very
likely you have ? "

" No, indeed ! " he answered eagerly.
" Never was a man more devoid of any

semblance of a reason for hurrying there. None of my relations expect me, or know that I have left India. Even if they did, I can't flatter myself that my presence would make any great difference to them. Indeed, were I to go to England to-morrow, I believe my first impulse would be to present myself at Mordaunt."

"Really. Then do let us have the benefit of it. I know grandmamma would spare you if she knew, and you can form no idea of what a boon your company would be to us. It is very selfish though, I know, to urge it," she went on penitently. "As Algernon says, we clutch at any friendly hand that comes in our way as if we were literally drowning. And to have *you* at hand would be—I really cannot tell you what it would be!"

The others were still a little behind, having stopped again to read an inscription. John Lawrence hesitated. Her last words had touched him deeply. Although his six years' heartache was, be believed, cured,

she was still and always must be the shrine
in which the love of his life lay buried. To
be of use to her he would have compassed
sea and land, and have sacrificed his own
comfort without a word or a second thought.
There was another side to the question,
however. His old dislike of Algernon
Cathers was still, he knew, alive, or had
been up to a very recent date. Could he,
even at this late hour, trust himself in his
company, seeing him daily, perhaps hourly,
without showing that dislike, which now
would be unseemly, nay, brutal to the last
degree. Had this piece of information
which he had just heard and the rush of
pity it had evoked effaced that dislike, or
was it still there, and liable to reappear at
any moment? If so, was he not bound in
honour to keep away?

Lady Eleanor looked a little surprised at
his hesitation. "I see what it is," she
said. "You are trying to arrange matters
so as to come with us, though there is
somewhere else you want to go, and it is

inconvenient to you to do so. Don't please, think of it. I spoke thoughtlessly. We are quite used to being stranded here when every one else is rushing home. It would be most unfair to insist upon detaining you after you have been so long away. You must want to get back to England, whether you have business there or not."

"I have nothing to do really," he answered earnestly. "And if I had I should far rather stay. It was not that that made me hesitate. The fact is I—I cannot quite decide immediately. If when you leave this I find that I can go where you are going, I will. If not, you will believe that it is not because other affairs, even if I had any, could count against your wishes. You believe that, don't you?"

"Yes, I believe it; I am sure you will come if you can," she answered. "I don't think I have ever disbelieved you, have I?" she added with a smile which woke the old Elly for an instant to his eyes. "You never gave me any cause, at any rate," she added more gravely.

CHAPTER III.

A COUPLE of mornings later he met her walking briskly along alone; her height, which lifted her several degrees above the general level of an Italian crowd, her fairness, and stately youthful beauty making her a sufficiently striking apparition to come upon in the crowded intricacies of a Genoese street. A dozen black moustaches and a couple of dozen eyes, ranging in social elevation from those of the umbrella-mender at the corner to those of an officer of carbineers, with cloak slung slantwise over his shoulder, were all concentrated in her direction, with that undisguised admiration which is Italy's tribute to beauty. That she was unconscious herself of that tribute,

was evident, but the Colonel, as he joined
her, was not equally unconscious, and he
glared right and left with a sense of pro-
prietary indignation for which he would
have found it rather difficult to find a
justification.

"I am shopping," she said, when they
had shaken hands. "I am on my way to
a carpet shop. We do most of the furnishing of our villa here, or rather try to do so.
Will you come with me? If you are sight-
seeing the carpet shop is worth a visit, as
you will see."

They passed down a narrow street into
the square of Bitter Fountains and through
it into the newly named Via Garibaldi,
passing between heavily-barred windows,
each as wide as the frontage of a moderate-
sized house; past staircases, guarded here
by a pair of gigantic lions, growling at
vacancy, there by a colossus brandishing
his club in the middle of a lonely courtyard. The crowd poured along; tramcars
trotted briskly over the pavement, driving

foot-passengers against the walls; overhead the grandest row of houses probably ever raised by human hands lifted their colossal roofs above the turmoil.

Lady Eleanor turned into the entrance of one of these; through a great vaulted hall and in by an incongruously modern glass door, which swung to with such rapidity that it was as much as the Colonel could do to catch and hold it for her. Inside, the old and the new Italy seemed to meet and confront one other. It was a vast echoing hall, populous, no doubt, with memories, had any one been there to supply a key; with windows set so high in the wall, that the sun might beat for ever without reaching the floor, and through which the turmoil they had left without came in faint and muffled reverberations, as to some deep-lying ocean cavern. The floor of the cavern was strewn, not with the bones of drowned men, but with bales upon bales of carpet, gorgeous to look upon, afflictive for the most part to the æsthetic eye. They abounded in orange

and green; in mauve and red; above all in
magenta and that crude purpureal blue
beloved by the Italy of to-day. Bunches
of impossible roses and lilies, tied with
still more impossible bows of ribbon, were
there in truly appalling contrast; English
manufactures for the most part, but English
manufactures whose market has of late
happily waned at home, but which appear
to have fallen in a variegated cataract upon
the devoted peninsula, to the delight of its
natives and the unspeakable woe of its
visitors. Tier above tier they ranged, and
between them hung rugs and door-mats of
the same gorgeously afflictive type, a
magnificent Bengal tiger stretched at
full length under a bottle-green palm-tree
depending from the ceiling, upon which a
Triumph of Venus—the work evidently of
no mean hand—might still be faintly seen
amongst cobwebs in the dim light reflected
off a neighbouring white-washed wall.

Colonel Lawrence seated himself upon a
roll of carpet, and looked at the ceiling,

while Lady Eleanor proceeded to explain her requirements to one of the officials of the establishment, who hurried out of an inside office to receive her orders. Presently she was carried off to inspect something in another room, and the colonel was left sitting on his bale of carpet under the supervision of a pair of clerks with beautiful pointed moustaches, whom, had he met elsewhere, he would probably have taken for a couple of youthful attachés. She came back after a while with an air of rather unsuccessful effort; thanked the official, who attended her with obsequious bows to the entrance, and they passed out again through the glass doorway into the street.

"It is so difficult to get what one wants," she said, in a tone of vexation. "Algernon has such a wonderfully correct eye that it is a misery to him to have to sit in any room where the furniture is not exactly what he wishes it to be. It was only the simplest thing I wanted—merely some quite common felt or matting of a good plain neutral tint. I see though that we shall not be able to get it here, and I must write therefore to Paris; the things that good man showed me with such pride would simply have given Algernon a fit! I used to think when I was a girl," she went on with a smile, " that anything was to be had if you liked to pay for it, but since I have been married I have learnt that that is a great mistake."

" Most things, I should have thought, if you went to the right places for them."

" Oh no, indeed, not even then! Not when you have a high standard: I have hardly any standard myself, so I am not a case in point; so long as things are not too obtrusively glaring or out of harmony I am satisfied. But Algernon has trained his eye to such a point of exactitude that nothing short of perfection satisfies him, and perfection is not to be attained, I assure you, by writing cheques. You must go yourself; you must be content

to take any amount of pains; to be as
careful, in short," she added with a smile,
" as if your carpet and curtains were so many
suitors for the hand of your daughter."

"Isn't it rather a mistake wearing out
your life over that sort of thing? After
all, the pleasure to be extracted out of
carpets and curtains, let them be what they
may, doesn't amount to much, does it?"

" Perhaps not, but don't let any one hear
you say so. They would simply set you
down once for all as a Philistine—a being
to be avoided. To tell the honest truth,"
she went on, " my own theory is that a
little bit of Philistinism in one's composition is rather a comfort than otherwise.
Your life runs smoother, and you are less
perpetually jarred and shocked by an un-
avoidable contact with ugliness. But that
is a heresy, not to be breathed except into
very discreet ears."

"I can understand *ladies* spending their
time over such things," the Colonel said in
his gruffest, most John-Bull-like tones;

"but not men; men have generally other things to do."

"Yes, but then you have admitted you are a Philistine, have you not? Besides, supposing you had not many other things to do, and supposing you were delicate, and had no profession, and a good deal of money to get through; supposing, too, you were born with a very artistic temperament, can't you imagine yourself growing hypercritical about such matters, insisting that you would have nothing short of perfection? Of course the Nemesis of taste, when it is cultivated up to a really high pitch, is that it never *can* be really satisfied. It always remains hopelessly behind its own ideal."

The Colonel did not answer. The allusion to her husband's health had sent his thoughts back to the conversation he had had two days before with Mr. Nokes at the Campo Santo. He was rather startled, therefore, when she presently added—

"How do you think him looking?"

"Your husband? He is paler than he

used to be, and—and thinner," he said
hesitatingly. " Otherwise I don't see any
great difference—at least, not much."

She shook her head.

" You are not speaking with your usual
candour. Don't be afraid of alarming me.
I know how much need of care there is
better than any one." She paused a
minute or two, and then went on with a
sort of passion. " The great difficulty—the
almost hopeless difficulty—is to find any
occupation that can really interest him—
that any one in his state of health can
pursue. You have no idea how hard it is
until you try. Of course, a clever active-
minded man like Algernon wearies of all
these places; of the idleness; the want
of any definite occupation, even of any
definite amusement. He is tired of Mentone, tired of the Riviera, tired of this place,
tired of Spezia, tired of Florence, yet he is
absolutely forbidden to return to England
before the beginning of June. Every day
I dread his proposing to do so. We went

last year, and the result was he got a chill which he has never entirely got over." She paused, and then went on again in a tone of beseeching urgency. " If you could help me in this, if you could support me and persuade him—without, of course, showing I had asked you to do so—to be prudent, to refrain from running risks, you don't know what it would be! That is what I want more than anything,—a friend, some one who is not a woman, nor yet a doctor. I know how unreasonable it is of me to ask it of you, but if you only *knew* the misery of having no one to consult, no one to share my responsibility. Will you?—for as long as you are with us—will you help me ? "

" I will try; I will do my best," John Lawrence answered curtly. So *this* was what he had come back from India for, was it? *This* was his unseen destiny, the work he was sent to do! he said to himself. Well, if it was to be, it was, and he would do what he could. She should not have it to say that she had asked him in vain !

They went into the hotel. As they were going upstairs a small voice was heard above, speaking with that shrill childish distinctness which always gives the hearer a peculiar sensation; a thin, vernal shrillness like the first piping notes of a very young bird.

"But Muddie thaid I might!"—then followed something indistinct in another voice, and then——"But Muddie thaid I might, and Muddie knowths."

A small pattering of feet, and little Jan appeared; first a pair of scarlet-stockinged legs; then her little elf-like face, with its crown of straw-coloured hair. After her, in full pursuit, followed a large, handsome woman, with black heavily-arched eyes, and a coarse but brilliant brunette complexion. Jan, however, had caught sight of her mother, and rushing down the next flight of stairs, was clasping her tightly round the knees.

" What is it, my darling ? " Lady Eleanor
said. " I hope you have not been naughty,
Jan ? "

" No, not naughty. Maddymoiselle thays
that I musthn't go to Muddie—not all day
—but I may, mayn't I Muddie ? "

Lady Eleanor glanced for an explanation
toward the woman who had now reached
the same level.

" I understood that Miladi desired *la
petite* should remain upstairs until she was
sent for," she answered volubly in French.
Her manner was perfectly respectful, but
there was something unpleasant, the
Colonel thought, about the expression of
her eyes.

" Did I ? I don't think I did. She
always comes to me at this hour," Lady
Eleanor said in a tone of some surprise.
" Go up, Jan dear, and finish your lessons
very well, and then Mademoiselle I am sure
will let you come down."

" What a good-looking woman ! " the
Colonel said, when they had gone on into

the sitting-room, which proved to be empty. " She is Italian, is she not ? "

" No. French, Provençal. She lives at Mentone, and has been coming to us every day this winter to teach Jan, and when we left to come here, she asked to accompany us."

" Have you known her long ? "

" Not very. Some friends of Algernon's had her as nursery governess for their children. She is a very good teacher. Unfortunately, Jan has taken rather a dislike to her, though she never will tell me why. And to tell the truth," she added, with a smile, " I rather share the feeling, though I, too, cannot tell you why. I always had a ridiculous wish to beg her not to look at me."

" Why do you keep her, if you dislike her ? " John Lawrence asked with some surprise.

" Well, it doesn't seem a sufficient reason for parting with her, does it ? Algernon, too, likes her and thinks she keeps Jan in order. I am afraid I am rather susceptible to likes and dislikes. When I was a child, you may remember, I was always devoted to or detested every one I came near, and I have not got over the tendency even yet. Mlle. Riaz is a capital teacher, there can be no question of that."

"Nevertheless I wouldn't have any one in the house whom I disliked," he answered. "You may be sure it is a mistake. The more so, as that sort of feeling is almost invariably returned."

"Do you really think so?" she said, in rather a startled tone.

"I am sure of it. And if the dislike is strong from above, think how much stronger it is likely to be from below—in the person, I mean, who has to receive orders, than in the person who gives them. Besides one never really keeps a feeling like that concealed, however hard one may try."

"It has sometimes struck me Mlle. Riaz did not like me," Lady Eleanor said, thoughtfully. "At least, she seems to like to cross my will about trifles—only, of course, about trifles. Her manner is always perfectly respectful. I was once very angry —unreasonably angry — with her about something, and I have felt mentally in an apologetic attitude towards her ever since."

"Then, if I were you I would find an opportunity of getting unreasonably angry again, and of giving Mlle. Riaz her *congé*," he said with a laugh.

"Don't say that. Nothing humiliates one like losing one's temper. I watch over mine as if it were a case full of diamonds. I would rather lose everything else I possess. People who have good tempers are enviable beyond words. Mine is very bad, and I don't believe it improves either, though I don't suppose I show it as much as I did when I was a child."

"Judging by looks your Mlle. Riaz has a temper too, a worse one than yours I suspect! Anyhow I wouldn't keep her if

I were you. I don't think a feeling of that sort comes for nothing."

"Perhaps not, and yet it doesn't seem fair that another person should be the sufferer by one's own fancies. Added to which I don't think Algernon would let me take any sudden step of the kind, at least without a better reason."

The door opened while she was still speaking and her husband came in.

"What wouldn't that domestic tyrant Algernon let you do?" he enquired with a smile and a nod of greeting to the visitor. He had a great bunch of orchids in his hands which he was smelling at luxuriously as he advanced.

His wife coloured a little. "We were only talking of Mlle. Riaz," she said. "I was saying that she is an excellent teacher, and that I wished I liked her better. It is so stupid to take dislikes for no particular reason."

Her husband was still smelling his orchids, but glanced over them at her with rather an odd expression. His voice, however, when he answered was carelessness itself.

" Oh, she is a very good sort of creature," he said, sitting down by a table and beginning to arrange the flowers. " One must pay some tribute to the country one lives in. We can't employ absolutely nothing but our own dear countrymen and countrywomen, can we? I am sure we have sufficiently vindicated our patriotism in that direction as it is. Take your Mrs. Peacock—for a starched-out piece of English propriety one could hardly go beyond her! She would chill the very sun out of the sky if she could get hold of it for the purpose. Talk of antipathy! that woman gives me the cold shivers every time she comes into the room. I feel as if a large piece of ice, or two or three frogs were slowly making their way down the middle of my spinal marrow ! "

Lady Eleanor looked vexed.

" Peacock has been with me ever since I was twelve years old, Algernon," she

said, rather hastily. "I should feel like
giving up one of my own relations if I sent
her away—without, of course, any very
urgent reason."

"Goodness, gracious, my dear, I know!
Don't imagine for an instant that I want
you to send her away. I thought we were
only talking in the abstract about our little
antipathies. I have mine as well as you
yours. It is much better than invariably
liking and disliking the same things.
Nothing makes domestic life so monoto-
nous, and goodness knows, we don't require
any aids in that direction!"

Lady Eleanor did not answer. The
Colonel began to think of taking leave.
Fortunately a diversion arrived just then
in the person of little Jan, her flaxen
hair sticking on end, her silk skirt corre-
spondingly elevated, her small face with its
serious responsible-looking eyes looking
soberly out between the two extensions.

Her father caught her by the arm as she
was crossing the room to go to her mother.

" Well, Miss Propriety, and how are you to-day?" he inquired.

" Quite well, thank you, father."

It was maintained in the family that Jan had never talked broken English in her life. She had kept a rigid silence until she was nearly three, when one fine day she broke it by a question delivered in unimpeach-able English. Whether the tale was true or not, there was no doubt that she spoke with an accuracy which the infant Macaulay might have envied, in spite of a lisp which she made the most heroic efforts to over-come. It followed that nothing offended her so much as to be addressed in baby language, or accused of baby peccadilloes— a trait which naturally made it amusing to do so.

" So, Miss Prim, and what mischief have *you* been getting into to-day?" her father went on teasingly. " Pulling small bro-ther's hair, or stealing sweeties? Eh?"

" I haven't, father!" Jan opened a pair of indignantly grey eyes, the only feature of her small face which bore any resemblance to her mother's.

"Not stealing sweeties out of my gold snuff-box? Oh, come, come, take care!"

"No, father, I'm 'thure I haven't."

"You're ''thure you haven't.' Come, think a little. Didn't you see I was behind you all the time, and saw you do it."

"You couldn't have theen me, father, for I didn't. Did I, Muddie?"

"Father is only joking, Jan."

"Joking? Nonsense; don't put such ideas into her head. Little girls who steal sweeties, and tell titty-waggers, must expect to be found out."

Jan's eyes were beginning to look suspiciously round, and her mouth to twitch; her little cheeks, too, had become red as fire. Evidently those angry passions of which her mother had been complaining in her own case were alive here too.

"I didn't theel them, and I'm not tellin' titty-waggers!" she said in her little shrill staccato, pulling at her father's hands in order to escape. " And you're a bad, naughty father to say so ; yeth you are. It ith *you* are telling titty-waggers ! " and again she tried convulsively to escape.

" Hullo, Miss Propriety ! Getting into a tantrum about nothing ! Look there ! Do you see that big man sitting on that chair ? He keeps a black bag on purpose to put little girls into, who get into tantrums, and steal sweeties, and tell their papas they tell titty-waggers. How should you like to be put in, and the bag tied up quite tight, and that man to carry you away in it, so that you'd never see any of us, mother nor nobody never again ? "

John Lawrence felt provoked. It was only a joke, but it did not strike him as a particularly good one. He hated children to be teased for nothing.

Lady Eleanor interposed.

" Please let her go, Algernon," she said. " She is really hurt at your thinking that she stole the sugar-plums. Do tell her that you were only joking."

"Joking! Do you wish me to perjure myself? The child would never believe me again! Now Jan; one, two, three! Say you're sorry, and then I'll let you go!"

"I'm not thorry, for I didn't. Muddie knowths I didn't!"

"Mother knowths, does she? Mother is very clever, but she wasn't there, so she can't know. Now listen to me. You're not going to be let go until you have said you're sorry. I'll give you three minutes more, and if you haven't said it then, into the black bag you go."

Jan again struggled, looking round for help as she did so. She was a very wise child, but she was not quite wise enough to be certain that the black bag was a myth, and she glanced at the reputed possessor of it with a glance that went to that good-natured personage's heart, and he made haste to clear himself of the odious suspicion.

"Never you mind what he says! They always say they haven't got the bag until they get you safely stowed inside it!" said her father. "Now then, Jan, two, three, four. Time's nearly up!"

But Jan only set her teeth and shut up her little lips, as if to hinder a word from slipping through. Her pride was evidently roused, and even with the black bag in prospect she would die before she surrendered.

"Say you're sorry for having been rude to father, dear," her mother said, getting up and going over to her.

But Jan had begun to sob, and was now past speaking.

"Let her go, please, Algernon," said her mother in a tone of entreaty. "She will make herself ill and not be able to sleep a wink to-night," she went on, beseechingly. "And it's so very bad for her temper too."

"Little kittens must learn to control their tempers then. Don't spoil sport, Eleanor. She was just going to give in when you interfered."

"But she really *will* make herself ill,

Algernon. You know what an excitable
child she is, and how she takes everything
to heart. *Do* let her go," Lady Eleanor
said earnestly, taking hold of one of her
husband's hands as she spoke, to enforce
her appeal.

John Lawrence had all the mind in the
world to go to her aid, but wisely refrained.
Indeed, it was unnecessary. Algernon
Cathers resisted, laughing the while at her
and himself. Finger by finger, however,
his grasp was unfastened. Suddenly Jan,
with a shrill cry of delight, escaped and fled
round to the other side of her mother,
grasping her skirts tenaciously with both
little liberated hands.

Her father made no effort to recapture
her. He was laughing still, but threw himself back in his chair, as if tired with the
struggle.

" Oh, if you choose to bring brute force
to bear upon discipline and moral training,
of course, they must go to the wall,"
he declared. " I never flattered myself

that I was a fit match — physically, at any rate—for your ladyship," he added meaningly.

Lady Eleanor did not answer. She was soothing little Jan, who still sobbed and clung convulsively to her skirts, as if in terror of being dragged away.

" Hush, hush, Jan! There, that will do! Don't cry any more, dear. It was only a joke. When you are a little older you will know the difference between joke and earnest."

Jan ceased sobbing. She was evidently a small person with a good deal of self-control. She still, however, clung to her mother, eyeing her father from behind that defence with an air of suspicion naturally not a little irritating to the latter.

" Pack her off to the nursery," he said, impatiently, turning to collect the flowers, which had got scattered over the table in the struggle. " Kittens that mew and scratch the minute they're touched must be put into their baskets and kept there! "

" Mlle. Riaz has gone out, but I will take her up to Peacock in a minute or two," his wife answered.

" Ah when she is with Mlle. Riaz nothing of this sort happens ! "

Meanwhile John Lawrence had got up to go.

" Going, Colonel ? " his host enquired. " This ' domestic and particular broil ' has been too much for you ! I assure you it doesn't happen every day. In fact, we never fight except over the kittens. Do we, Eleanor ? Come and dine with us this evening, and you will see. The kittens will be safe upstairs in their baskets then."

But John Lawrence replied rather gravely that he couldn't he was afraid dine that evening.

" To-morrow, then ? Have you a friendly heart in your bosom, and can you resist our appeal ? Here I am tied by the leg to this ' doleful, dolorous, midland sea '—never was a truer description ! and the only alleviation is the occasional sight of a new face, and a fresh ear to pour my complaints into. As a friend of peace, if in no other character, you ought to come. If I have no other resource I must fall back upon the time-honoured Briton's right of tormenting my wife and family. What other occupation have I? Persuade him, Eleanor."

"Do please come to-morrow," she said earnestly. "You will be giving us the very greatest pleasure."

"There you see! she expects you to intervene between her and her natural tyrant. Can you refuse?"

"Thanks, if you are sure it really suits you I shall be happy to come to-morrow," the Colonel answered rather formally.

He had already shaken hands with Lady Eleanor, and now moved toward the door, Algernon Cathers getting politely up to open it. As the latter was leaving the table, he again caught up the great odoriferous bunch of orchids, and held it lovingly to his nose. This time, however, something was wrong apparently with the scent, or it was different from what he expected, for with a grimace, and a gesture expressive of humorous disgust, he suddenly tossed the whole brightly coloured bunch bodily into an empty fireplace.

END OF VOL. II.